W9-ANI-637

SHADOWBOXER

SHADOWBOXER

by

Mark A. Calde

G. P. PUTNAM'S SONS
New York

SBN: 399-11799-7

Library of Congress Cataloging in Publication Data
Calde, Mark A 1945–
Shadowboxer.

I. Title.
PZ4.C142Sh [PS3553.A3946] 813'.5'4 76-8278

PRINTED IN THE UNITED STATES OF AMERICA

To my wife, Shelley

Acknowledgments

There is always an endless list of individuals who provide support when someone is crazy enough to wake up one morning and announce that he is going to write a novel. To all of them—my family and wonderful friends—I say a heartfelt "thanks." And on the professional side of the ledger, I owe a large debt of gratitude to Mel Dir for his thoughtful and invaluable assistance.

1

Harry Milford stood panting, trying desperately to catch his breath. He put his hands on his hips and leaned back to gulp in air. It rushed down his throat, clogged in the overworked bellows of his lungs, and he almost retched. He doubled over and put his head between his knees to keep from passing out. Slower, he thought. Don't be greedy. Take the time you need. But he knew he couldn't. He calculated he had perhaps thirty seconds, maybe less, before he'd have to begin running again. His chest throbbed, and his legs were like two numb foreign objects that had been thrust into the trunk of his body. Yet he had to keep moving. It was run or be caught. Life had been reduced to its basics. Survive or perish. The choice was his.

He straightened up. Breathing was easier now. A muted rumbling droned on in the background. He wished to hell he could identify it. It seemed so familiar.

Brushing a shock of dark hair from his eyes, he felt the salty sting of sweat on his cracked lips. Then, looking over his shoulder, he saw them coming. They were perhaps a hundred yards away, their hazy outlines bobbing up and down against the backdrop of the vague landscape. They'd been running as long as he had, but they never seemed to tire. Why? Were they trained for this sort of thing?

Enough, he told himself. Theorize while you're moving, or you'll be caught. And killed.

Harry put his legs into motion. They obeyed him grudgingly. What was this muck he was running in? Traction was almost impossible. His footing gave way every five or six strides, making a farce of his efforts to sustain any kind of rhythm. But wouldn't it be the same for his pursuers? He tried to tell himself it would, yet somehow he felt that they suffered none of his handicaps. For them it was a stroll through the park, not a lung-bursting, pain-ridden ordeal. Their goal was in sight; they had nothing to worry about. It was simply a matter of time until he dropped.

Faster. He had to go faster. The gap was closing; he could feel it, and he was afraid to glance back and confirm his fear. His eyes strained through the sweat that blurred his vision. Was that an outcropping of vegetation ahead? Were those formless shapes really trees that offered concealment and another chance to rest before being forced once again into the chase? No, he decided, they were only the tricks of the sun playing on his tired, confused mind.

His labored breathing was accompanied by the constant muted rumbling somewhere off to his right. The sound was infuriating, but like an elusive name, it remained just out of his grasp.

Think, Milford. Wipe your mind clean of everything but that damn sound. Pin a name to it. You've heard it before, a thousand times. Maybe it carries your salvation.

Nothing. He felt the frustration course through his body. Something was out there, something that he knew, and yet he couldn't identify it. What if it were a highway, teeming with cars. That would account for the rumbling noise. Of course. If it were a highway, it would offer traction to his blistering feet. It would lead to civilization and, most important, his pursuers wouldn't dare lay a hand on him in full view of passing motorists.

He smiled cynically to himself. People were killed all the time in full view of dozens of other people, and no one ever lifted a hand to intervene. Why should he be something special? Why should anyone bother to get involved in order to help Harry Milford? Maybe he should just turn and run pointblank into the sound. At least, that way if it were really a highway he'd have the chance of being obliterated by a car. With any luck, it should be almost entirely painless. Just the shock of the impact, and then . . .

His left foot thudded into a jagged rock, and the pain shot up his leg and into his groin. He pitched headfirst to the ground, his body attempting an awkward somersault before coming to rest.

Harry lay on his back staring up at what should have been the sky but was instead a limitless expanse of dirty brown haze. He hoisted himself up on one elbow and began gingerly to probe his left leg for any signs of fracture. As far as he could tell, nothing was broken. But he knew that the test of weight was the crucial one. Slowly, putting all the stress on his right leg, he stood up. Then, as gently as he could, he gradually began to equalize his weight. He was just beginning to feel that he was going to be all right when the leg suddenly gave and the shooting pain returned. It threw him off-balance, and as he felt himself sinking toward the ground, everything seemed to lapse into slow motion. It was at that moment that he saw them advancing. They were closing the distance with smooth, workmanlike strides—no more than fifty yards away now.

He hit the ground, and the true tempo of his senses returned. He had to get moving. In a few moments they'd be upon him. But he wouldn't be taken as a beaten man. They'd have to catch him, by God.

Once again he struggled to his feet, and once again the pain flung him back down. He hoisted himself up onto his forearms and began a belly-crawl.

He could hear them now, hear the sound of their footfalls. They were running evenly, without strain. His elbows dug into the ground, and he dragged his body along as fast as he could. He began to count, telling himself they'd have him before he reached twenty. But it didn't matter. Because when the first hand was laid on his shoulder, he was still going to keep moving. If they wanted him to stop moving, they were going to have to knock him unconscious. Then, hopefully, he would never wake up.

Eighteen, nineteen, twenty. Silence.

That was when the real fear entered Harry. They should have had him by then, but they didn't, and he couldn't hear them anymore.

He crawled on, his eyes two stinging slits from the sweat that poured off his face.

Twenty-six, twenty-seven, twenty-eight. Where the hell were they? Thirty-one, thirty-two . . .

Harry Milford stopped crawling.

His burning eyes saw. The foggy mass of his mind comprehended. His face was approximately three inches from a man's leg. It stood erect, and his blurry gaze followed its vertical plane up to a torso. He had a fuzzy vision of two massive arms folded across a chest—an unmistakable gesture of finality. He rolled over on his back and saw that they had encircled him. There were five of them, and they stood in identical fashion: legs apart and arms folded. He tried to focus on their faces, but for some reason they appeared as only shadowy blotches above five sets of shoulders.

Harry made a move to get up, but his leg wouldn't allow it. Then they began to close in on him, slowly drawing the circle tighter and tighter. He had no choice but to lie there and watch it happen.

Now they were bending over him, arms extended, hands groping down toward him. The muted rumbling continued in the background. He opened his mouth to shout an obscenity, but before he could utter a syllable, he was assailed by an earsplitting, high-pitched screech that originated from somewhere far above him. Then, in the midst of his final moments, he heard something that he simply didn't believe possible.

He could have sworn it was the sound of a piece of china shattering on the hard surface of a floor.

2

"Damn!" Carol Milford cursed the broken plate on the kitchen floor. In the small den a few steps away, Harry lay on the Leatherette sofa trying to banish the icy ball of fear in his stomach. He glanced at the doorway as Carol entered.

"Did I wake you?" she asked. "I'm sorry."

A wave of his hand indicated it didn't matter. "What broke?"

"Oh, another plate," she said disgustedly. "The floral pattern. That puts us down to five in that set."

He swung his lean, six-foot frame around to a sitting position. "Don't worry about it. We never really cared for them anyway." He was glad she'd broken the plate. It had saved him.

"How's your headache?"

"Better," he said. "Do I have time for a drink before dinner?"

"Sure. It'll be about fifteen minutes yet. Provided I don't break anything else."

They smiled at each other, and she returned to the kitchen. He watched the pleasant movement of her body as she walked away. Even in an apron she looked good. He'd always been proud of his wife's appearance. She was attractive in a smart, understated way. All her features—her light-blond hair (which was natural), her not-too-full breasts, her shapely legs, her soft-blue eyes—melded together unobtrusively to form a warm, comfortable picture.

Harry stood up and gently massaged his temples, grateful

that the pain was finally diminishing. He'd never been prone to headaches, and when this one had hit on the way home from the office, it had struck with vicious force, like razor blades tearing through his brain.

He walked to the oak liquor cabinet that stood in the dining room and mixed himself a stiff Scotch and water. As he swirled the ice cubes in the amber liquid, he could hear Carol in the kitchen preparing dinner. Though they'd been married for almost ten years—ten good years—and though they'd confided in each other freely during that time, he still hesitated to tell her what was happening to him. The reason for his hesitation was a simple one: he didn't *know* what was happening to him.

He moved into the living room, sat down in his favorite chair, took a long pull on his drink, and tried to sort things out.

Things? There was really only one thing. The nightmare. And this was the third day in a row that it had plagued him, always the same. He was being chased across that vague, indistinguishable landscape, accompanied in his flight by a low, muted rumbling that he couldn't identify, even though it seemed maddeningly familiar. He was running for his life, but he didn't know why. What had he done? Why were they after him? None of it made any sense.

And in the end, he was always caught. Helpless, he would wait for death. Then the high-pitched screech would knife through the scene, bringing with it a return to reality. Reality, however, offered little salvation. His eyes would be open, his body would be in the present, but his mind would still be back there, trapped and waiting to die. Even now, as he sat in the comfort of his own living room drinking Scotch and listening to the reassuring sounds coming from the kitchen, he could still feel the grip of the dream on his thoughts. In fact, for the last three days he'd never really been able to shake it. Not completely. He didn't like to admit that to himself, but he knew it was true.

He took another pull on his drink and waited for the liquor

to do its work. What about the headache? Was that another symptom? Harry tried to discount it, chalk it up to coincidence. No good. He knew damn well he didn't get headaches. Oh, maybe once a year if he were coming down with the flu—but to be feeling fine and suddenly get hit with a raging monster like that? No. It wasn't his style. His body had never before played tricks like that on him. So why should it start now?

A thought raced through his mind. A single word that carried chilling implications. Tumor.

What if something were growing inside his skull, pressing against the tissue of his brain, preparing to slowly choke out all the functions that distinguished him as a human being? He had a terrible vision of himself as a flaccid hulk neatly stored between clean white bedsheets. That was certainly nothing he could call a man—a burden to Carol, a constant drain on the few dollars they'd put away, a thing to be washed and turned and fed through a tube.

Stop it, Milford. The next thing you know, you'll be fantasizing your own eulogy. So you've had a persistent bad dream and a headache. Big deal. It'll pass. It started by itself, and it'll finish by itself, and that's all there is to it.

He tried to tell himself that that was the commonsense answer to his problem. Yet, somehow he knew that whatever was taking hold of him was certainly far from common.

"Dinner, honey." Carol's voice was a pleasant intrusion into his thoughts. Harry downed the last of his drink and made his way into the dining room.

His wife was lifting a portion of egg noodles onto each plate. In the center of the table, a chafing dish held a dark, bubbling mixture that gave off a steady vapor of steam and an appetizing aroma of white wine.

"Smells good," he said as he sat down.

"I hope so. It's a new recipe. Sue gave it to me. She swears by it and says it's *the* genuine way to do Stroganoff."

Carol passed him his plate and finished serving herself.

"Your headache still on its way out?" she asked.

"Almost gone," he lied. The pain was still there. Not the raging fury it had been before the nightmare, but bad enough to make him wish he'd taken some aspirin instead of the Scotch.

"Are you sure you aren't coming down with something? You never get headaches."

"It's nothing. It'll go away." He speared a cube of meat on his fork and held it above his plate, letting it cool. He felt uncomfortable, as if he were on display at his own dinner table. Absurd. Why should he feel like that? He placed the meat in his mouth; it was still too hot and burned his tongue.

"How is it?" Carol asked. "Be honest. I can always scramble some eggs if it isn't any good."

"It's fine. Really delicious."

"Good. It's so embarrassing when a friend gives you a recipe and you have to lie about it."

"We're seeing them soon, aren't we?"

"The Martins? Tomorrow night. They're coming over after dinner for drinks."

"That'll be fun," he said, and hoped he sounded like he meant it, because he really did. Phil and Sue Martin were their next-door neighbors and probably the best friends they had, given the fact that Harry and Carol had lived in the small Maryland suburb for only six months. Harry was a government employee. He'd met his wife in Washington, D.C., and they'd spent the first nine years of their marriage there. Then came the transfer to the sprawling new agency in Maryland. At the time, he'd been given only the vaguest of reasons for the move, but a career with the government presupposes vagueness, and he'd accepted the decision with a minimum of regret. So had Carol. In fact, he'd been slightly perplexed at her readiness to pack up and go, but she'd been all eagerness and expectation and had handled the moving details flawlessly. Most wives would have made it an ordeal.

"You haven't heard a word I've been saying, have you?" Her voice brought his wandering thoughts back to the present.

"Sorry about that. I was daydreaming."

"Anything exciting?"

"Just our moving here, how helpful the Martins were. Things like that."

"I'll never forget that first night—nothing but unpacked boxes everywhere we looked. Then the doorbell rang and there were Sue and Phil with a bottle of champagne to welcome us to the neighborhood." She smiled, half in embarrassment. "It went straight to my head. I never got so high so fast in all my life."

The two of them laughed softly, sharing the moment together.

"And somehow," she continued, "you managed to dig out the portable radio, and we all danced to the music on that crazy station you found."

Harry opened his mouth to say something, but the words never came. The pain shot through his skull with staggering force. The color drained from his face in a matter of seconds.

Carol reached her hand across the table toward him. "Harry, what's the matter? What happened?"

He forced himself to speak, hoping desperately that his voice retained at least a semblance of normalcy. "It's just the headache, that's all. Nothing a couple of aspirin can't handle."

"I'll get them," she said. "You sit still." The concern in her tone was obvious, and she was gone from the room before he could say anything else.

Then, as quickly as it had come, the agony abated. It seemed as if he literally felt it drain out from his head. By the time Carol returned with the aspirin and a glass of water, she could see that he was feeling better. Silently she held out her open hand with the chalky-white pills and watched as he swallowed them. He set the half-drained water glass down on the table and looked up at her.

"It's better now," he said. "It really is."

He wanted her to answer quickly, but she didn't. Instead, she gave him a long, quiet look. He'd never seen her face quite like that before. He thought he saw a kind of sad resignation beneath the love and worry. And oddly, it bothered him.

"I think you should see a doctor," she said softly.

"No. I don't need a doctor. I'll be fine."

She pressed his hand between hers. "Okay." Her voice was barely audible. "We'll do it your way."

3

"You'll have your own office." That was the most concrete thing they'd told Harry seven months ago when they'd informed him of his transfer to the Maryland agency. That and the fact that he and Carol would have thirty days to complete the move. (The government would buy their Washington home from them, cash.)

He looked around his "office"—a windowless ten-by-twelve area with olive-green, three-quarter plastic partitions separating it from the neat rows of desks that filled the rest of the massive room. Two beige vinyl chairs with walnut-grain arms and spindly aluminum legs sat empty across from him, a brass-colored cigarette stand between them. His desk was a gray metal affair that was always cold to the touch. The pencil cup, Tensor lamp, digital clock, Daily Reminder pad, and framed photo of Carol that were spread across the surface did little to warm its appearance. Typical government-issue surroundings to complement his typical government-issue life.

His job consisted of reading reports already read and duly initialed by others, evaluating his co-workers' written comments, and composing a definitive summary of them. He would then pass the documents on to his superiors for final analysis, and they, in turn, would forward the reports for microfilming, after which all written copies, together with their attendant memos and addenda, would be fed into the shredder and carted away at the end of each day to be recycled and eventually return as blank white pages waiting to be filled with more reports.

The six months that he'd spent there had slid by unobtrusively, the victims—like everything else—of routine. Ordinarily, he wouldn't have cared. But these weren't ordinary times; the events of the past three days had seen to that. Now, as he sat in his cubicle and stared down at the pages of print that rested on his desk, he strongly resented the passing of six months out of his life like so much sand through a child's fingers. Time was no longer an unlimited currency. He felt certain his supply was running short, just as he felt certain that he would rest his head on the pillow this evening and dream the dream again. The infernal dream. The dream that he somehow knew held the answer to his fate.

Harry sighed and glanced at the digital clock. It showed four fifty-three. He forced his eyes to begin scanning the print of the open report.

Abruptly, an involuntary tremor shook his body. His vision blurred, and he felt the pain begin to creep up the back of his neck. He shut his eyes tightly, but when he opened them, his focus was still distorted. Trying to control his panic, he pulled open the center drawer of his desk and fumbled for the tin of aspirin. He extracted two and eased himself to his feet, wondering all the time if his balance would be affected. It wasn't, and he moved gratefully toward the opening in the partitions.

By the time he'd reached the water cooler, the pain had spread to the top of his head and was beginning to travel down to his temples. Fortunately it wasn't too intense, and he hoped for relief as he popped the medication into his mouth.

What he got was terror.

As he stood there washing the pills down with a cone-shaped cup of cool water, his vision suddenly cleared and an image flashed across his sight line. It was so fleeting as to be almost subliminal, and like the events in the nightmare, it was a fragment of something severed totally from any meaningful context. The image was a numbered bank of lights, all of them unlit except for the number twenty-two, which glowed bright red.

The apparition came and went in the space of perhaps a single moment, but Harry had lived that moment with all his senses.

Behind him, the rustle of the office staff signaled that quitting time was near. He crumpled the paper cup and tossed it into the wastebasket, determined not to betray his fear when he turned around and walked back to his office.

The shelter of the green partitions was comforting as he slumped into his chair. His vision was still clear, and he found himself waiting expectantly for the image to reappear. But nothing came. He leaned his elbows on his desk and rested his head in his open palms. What had happened to him out there by the water cooler? Why was his life being interrupted with pain and nightmare and hallucination? What small, nameless part of him had suddenly failed four days ago and left him vulnerable to attack?

The questions tumbled one over the other through his mind. He remembered having read somewhere that the average adult brain weighed about five pounds, with the functions of a large portion of it still medically uncharted. That was where the answer must lie. Somewhere along the line the delicate circuitry must have frayed. He thought of a chain stitch that held the hem of a garment—one snip with the scissors, and all the links would dissolve with a single, steady tug on the thread, leaving a raw, unfinished edge.

Insanity.

Click. A new digit rolled into place on his desk clock. It was a few minutes past five, time to be leaving. His head throbbed. He stood and retrieved his suit jacket from the coat rack in the far corner of the cubicle. His vision was still clear, and he kept telling himself that the aspirin would be working by the time he got home.

The bite of the cool night air felt good against his face. As he made his way across the asphalt parking lot, he tried to steer a course away from anyone he knew, anyone who might say a casual good night and realize at once that something was terribly wrong.

He reached his car safely and shut himself inside its protective cocoon. An instant later the engine turned over, and he backed out of the parking space. The stenciled white arrows pointed the way to the exit, and soon the highway stretched in front of him.

Harry switched on the radio in an effort to divert his thoughts, but his pounding headache was only intensified by the pulse of the music, and he quickly turned it off. Rolling down the window, he began to take deep breaths of the damp evening air. It helped to calm him. The dashboard clock read five-twelve. In another ten minutes he'd be pulling into his driveway. The idea of stepping in the front door of his home and seeing Carol carried with it an extreme urgency. Deliberately he edged his speed to five miles over the legal limit. His left hand clenched and unclenched around the steering wheel while his right held firm. Nervously he glanced in the rearview mirror for any sign of a patrol car. All he saw was the tree-lined road receding behind him.

Then suddenly the entire scene was blotted out.

The area behind his car vanished, and in its place appeared the bank of lights with the number twenty-two still glowing a bright, ruby red.

As before, the image was a mere flash in his consciousness. Harry stared out the windshield and pressed his foot down on the accelerator. Then he reached through his panic and slowed to the speed limit. The last thing he wanted was to be stopped by the police. They'd take one look at him and start asking all sorts of questions. And he didn't have any answers.

The image came again, this time at a rakish angle. It was gone in the blink of an eye.

How many minutes to home? Seven, maybe eight. Just keep the car under control and don't attract any attention. The thoughts flowed desperately through the pain in his head. The image returned once more. And again. The intervals between were no more than a few seconds each. Then, as he rounded a gentle bend in the highway, he was attacked by a second apparition—bells ringing in a steeple. They clanged remorselessly. He *heard* them! He actually *heard* them, and they amplified the pounding in his skull.

Now the images were intersecting one another, leaving him precious little time to view the road ahead. Harry was being bombarded. He thought his head would split from the sound of the bells. The flashes were so close together now that he might as well have been driving with his eyes closed. Completely disoriented, he groped for the brake pedal to slow his speed.

The bank of lights. The bells. The bells. The bank of lights. Then a new sound. A sound from the real world. The throaty blast of a truck horn.

Harry swerved the wheel to the right and felt the tires hit the soft shoulder of the road as a fully loaded logging truck roared by, its air horn shattering even the agony of the bells.

4

The car rested docilely along the side of the road. Inside, Harry sat mesmerized by the speedometer, its thin red needle pointing at zero. Twilight was enveloping the trees. A fallen leaf slid gently down the windshield.

The panic was gone now, replaced by the unnatural calm of defeat. Somewhere in the back of his mind he felt a twinge of sadness at his frailty, but it was as if he were viewing it from a detached standpoint, like a grown child watching the advancing symptoms of age in his parents and telling himself over and over again that it happens to everyone, a physical inevitability that must be accepted.

He didn't remember turning off the engine, yet he was glad he'd been able to perform at least a minor rational act in the midst of his—what should he call it?—attack? The term brought a cynical response from him. Attacks, like accidents and terminal disease, were things that happened only to others. They were the stuff of newspaper articles and solemn pronouncements over martinis before the conversation turned to livelier topics. When he thought of the word as applying to himself, he found it difficult to digest—but not impossible. Because he knew that he *was* being attacked, that his sanity was suddenly beginning to erode and it was just a matter of time until the orderly process of his life would lie in rubble at his feet. Suddenly he felt overwhelmingly sorry for himself. All the pleasant years were coming to an end. Then, willfully, he pushed the pity from his mind. He couldn't afford such luxuries. Resolutely he turned the key in the ignition and eased out onto the highway. He was the prisoner of an unknown timetable, feeling his way blindly toward a hidden conclusion, and he couldn't help but wonder what would be waiting for him when he reached the end of the line.

By the time he swung the car into the driveway, he was determined not to tell Carol of the image flashes or the near-miss with the logging truck. Of course, he realized that he couldn't carry on the deception indefinitely, but until the obvious overruled him, each day that she didn't know what was happening to him would be one less day for her to suffer.

However, as soon as he walked through the front door and said hello she knew something was wrong. She came quickly out of the kitchen and met him in the living room.

"Honey? Everything okay?"

"Sure. Why not?"

"Don't try to fool me, Harry. I could hear it in your voice, and I can see it on your face. Something's bothering you."

He silently cursed his ineptitude and tried his best to be convincing.

"You know me too well." He smiled.

"If I don't by now, I never will. So out with it."

He gave an awkward shrug. "Just another headache, that's all."

"Again? When did it start?"

"This evening, before I left the office."

"I'm going to call Sue and cancel tonight."

"No, don't. Please. The company'll do me good. Besides, I took some aspirin before I left, and I'm feeling better already."

"You don't sound very convincing."

"Humor me. All right?"

"If you'll humor me and see a doctor," she said.

"Let's give it a little time. I can always see a doctor."

She stepped up to him and slid her arms around his waist. "I'm worried, Harry."

"Hey, come on. Everybody gets headaches."

"Not you. You know that."

"Honey, believe me, if it gets to the point where I have to see a doctor about it, I will."

"Promise?"

"I promise." He drew her close to him and kissed her gently on the top of the head. "Now, what's for dinner?"

Their conversation was animated all during the meal, each trying to ignore the tension present in the other. Afterward he helped her clear the table and then went to the bedroom to change while she filled the dishwasher.

As he pulled on a navy-blue turtleneck sweater, he glanced nervously at his watch. The Martins were due in fifteen or twenty minutes, and he was anxious for them to arrive, hungry for a chance at diversion. He hoped they'd stay late, allowing him to plead fatigue to Carol once they were gone; then, in the morning a vague excuse would limit breakfast to a quick cup of coffee and he'd be off to work, having avoided those uncomfortable minutes alone with Carol.

He sat down on the edge of the bed and felt ashamed that he was planning ways of avoiding his wife. He tried to rationalize it by saying he was protecting her, but that was a lie. He knew damn well the only one he was trying to protect was himself, because he was afraid of the moment when he would have to tell her that he was unsure how much longer his mind would last, afraid of the look of pity that would spring to her eyes, afraid of how he would react when the truth was finally out in the open. Until then, there was always the chance that the pain and hallucinations might not return. If ignorance was bliss, then self-delusion was at the very least a welcome limbo, a brief reprieve from an acknowledgment that would end the life he knew.

"Feeling better?" she asked as she entered the room.

"Feeling fine." And he really was. The headache was gone, and there were no mysterious images invading his world. He was just Harry Milford, government employee, waiting to begin an evening with friends.

"You know, if you want to cut things short tonight, don't stand on ceremony for Sue and Phil. They'd be the first to understand."

"Don't worry about it," he said. "Let's just relax and enjoy the evening. Okay?"

"I don't see how I can enjoy the evening if you're not feeling well."

"I already told you I was fine; what do you want from me?"

She'd been brushing her hair, and stopped in mid-stroke at his reply. "I want you to be honest with me, Harry. That's all."

"It's a little difficult when you won't believe anything I tell you."

"I never said that."

"You didn't have to—the way you stood there and looked at me like I was a little kid making up a story so I could go to a party."

"All right," she said calmly, "you're in the best shape of your life. That's obviously why you're acting like this."

"Would it make you happier if I said my head was still splitting and I was seeing things?"

"What do you mean, 'seeing things'?" The impatience had gone from her voice and was replaced by anxiety. Harry paled at his slipup, and his mind raced for a way to change the subject.

"Listen, I'm sorry I blew up like that. There was no excuse for it."

She nodded almost imperceptibly. "Now, tell me about the hallucinations."

"There aren't any. It was just a figure of speech."

"Was it?"

"Please, Carol, don't start again."

"I could say the same for you."

"I'm telling you the truth. There are *no* hallucinations."

She looked at him steadily, her eyes searching his face for any signs of betrayal.

"All right," she finally said. "I believe you."

"Good. Then I'll go get the ice and mixes ready. They'll be here soon."

Harry turned and left the room, and as he walked down the hallway, through the living room, and into the kitchen, a single thought repeated itself over and over again in his mind: She knew he was lying.

The doorbell rang at ten minutes past eight, and soon the room was filled with warm greetings, and the evening was underway.

"Give you a hand with the drinks?" Phil asked after Harry had taken everyone's order and was moving toward the kitchen.

"I never refuse an offer of help," Harry called back over his shoulder. "You know where I hide the booze," he said as he reached down four glasses from the overhead cabinet.

"Make mine a double," Phil said, setting the Scotch and bourbon bottles down on the counter next to the glasses.

"One of those days, huh?"

"One of those *weeks.* And it's only Wednesday. How's the United States government treating you?"

"No complaints."

"You're lucky. Look at this." Phil slapped the definite beginnings of a paunch that creased the waistband of his plaid trousers. "Ten pounds in a little over a month. Do you believe it? And all from pressure, pure and simple."

"You ought to slow down your pace a little."

"Tell that to my VP of sales. 'Third-quarter profits are down,' he says. So whose aren't? People are buying less these days. Everybody knows that. And what's his answer? 'Jack up those orders, Phil. That's your job.' How the hell can I jack up the goddamned orders if nobody has any money to spend? Will you answer me that?"

"Have a drink." Harry handed him a frost-encircled glass. "And here's Sue's."

"I better not get 'em mixed up, or she'll be out like a light in side of half an hour. Real big drinker, my wife."

As the two men entered the room, drinks in hand, Harry couldn't help noticing an abrupt change in the conversation between Carol and Sue.

"What are you two girls plotting now?" he asked as casually as he could.

"Not a thing," Sue answered almost too quickly. "Just some gossip you wouldn't be interested in."

"I'll get some coasters," Carol said, and was moving across the room before Harry could pursue the conversation without feeling awkward.

Phil handed Sue her drink, and Carol passed around the coasters and paper cocktail napkins printed with jokes that had ceased being funny years ago.

"Cheers," Harry said. He raised his glass with the others and tipped it to drink. As he did so, the ice cubes clinked harmlessly against the side of the glass.

Only, they weren't ice cubes. And the sound they made was anything but harmless.

He knew the look on his face must have been totally inexplicable, and he stammered some hasty words of cover. "Guess I didn't get enough water in mine. Be right back."

In the safety of the kitchen he set the glass down on the counter and stared at the ice floating lazily in the Scotch.

The bells. That's what they'd been. Less than ten seconds ago, in his own living room, in the presence of his wife and their best friends, those frozen cubes of water had contacted with the side of his glass and triggered a flash of the bells ringing in the tower. He'd seen them and heard them, just as he had while driving home from work, except that then he'd been alone, and now there were three people—three people who would be almost impossible to fool—waiting for him to return.

He quickly emptied the glass into the kitchen sink and then realized it was a mistake. He couldn't go back out there without a drink; that would bring an admission that he wasn't feeling well, and a quick end to the evening.

What, then? There was only one thing to do. Try to carry on as if everything were normal. Get himself back into the living room and into a chair and wait for whatever was coming next—but keep the Martins there as long as possible. If he was going to break down before the night was over, he wanted Carol to have some help around when it happened.

How much easier it would have been, he thought, if he'd met that logging truck head-on.

He picked up the stainless-steel tongs and gingerly lifted a cube from the ice bucket. He hesitated as he suspended it over the glass. Then he released the pressure on the tongs and let it drop.

Again the bells pealed frantically in the tower.

Then silence, and he was returned to his kitchen and the mocking cube of ice in the bottom of the glass. Quickly he shoveled more cubes in. His head rang with reverberations. He sloshed in some Scotch and turned on the faucet for water.

At that moment another enemy rose to greet him.

The sound of the running water caused a new image to flash before his eyes: it was an elaborate fountain, sending its multicolored jets of water high into the air before they fell in a million droplets into the waiting pool below.

Harry stood shaken, drink in hand. How many more fragments of this mental shrapnel would bombard him before it was all over? And when the end arrived, would he be condemned to wander forever in that bizarre new world that he only glimpsed now?

Frightened, he sighed and walked toward the swinging door that separated him from his wife and friends.

The three of them glanced up as he came in. Phil was in the process of polishing off a handful of peanuts, but Sue and Carol looked at him with what he was sure was pity, as if they knew the reason behind the terrible things that were happening to him. For a split second he came very close to bringing it all out in the open. "All right," he almost said, "tell me what's wrong. I'd rather know now and get it over with." But he stopped himself, because, of course, they couldn't know what was going on. Could they? No, they weren't doctors. Don't get paranoid, now, Harry thought to himself. So you're scared, but don't turn irrational. Keep a hold on yourself.

He made his way to a striped velvet armchair, expecting his sight line to be obliterated at every step by the clanging bells or the elaborate fountain or that inexplicable bank of numbered lights he'd seen during the drive home.

Nothing happened.

Harry sank gratefully into the chair as if it were some shelter where he could be free of the stalking enemy.

"Have some dip and join the party," Phil said as he plunged a potato chip into a garlicky cream-cheese mixture.

"Is your drink all right now?" Carol asked. She was doing a poor job of hiding her concern, and he knew it must be obvious to the Martins.

"I made a fresh one," he replied in what he hoped was a conversational tone. Then he raised his glass to his lips and winced involuntarily.

The bell tower stood unmercifully before him, then was gone.

"Something wrong?" Sue asked.

"The liquor just doesn't taste right to me tonight."

"Let me get you a Seven-Up or something," Carol said.

"Maybe that's a good idea," he said, and Carol was up and on her way out of the room.

Sue dabbed nervously at her dark-brown hair and fingered the buttons on her blouse that hung loosely over her small-breasted figure. The tension in the air was palpable. The evening was falling apart, and there was nothing Harry could do to stop it.

"We loved your Stroganoff recipe," he said lamely.

"Carol told me she'd tried it. I'm glad it worked out."

Silence hung heavily over the three of them, punctuated only by the occasional crunch of a potato chip between Phil's teeth. Then Carol was back, standing next to Harry and handing him a Seven-Up in a tall glass. He reached out for it but saw only the damnable tower, its bells tolling louder than ever before. He groped for the glass and missed it, then felt its icy surface and forced some of the cold liquid into his mouth, the carbonation stinging his throat. As he drank, he closed his eyes, preferring darkness to a sighted environment that he couldn't trust.

When he opened them, the multicolored fountain played where his wife and friends should have been. He waited for the image to leave, but it lingered tauntingly—three, four, five seconds. During that time he tried to set down his glass, but left it tottering on the edge of a cocktail table, where it tumbled immediately into his lap.

The shock of the ice-cold drink against his skin drove the image away, and he was met with the embarrassed stares of the others. He sat there for a moment like a clumsy, awkward child. Then he made the obligatory effort to salvage the situation.

"Just isn't my night, I guess." His voice sounded pitiful even to himself.

Carol was already retrieving the overturned glass. "I'll get this with a damp rag. You'd better go and change."

"Into a large bib," he tried to joke, but the words just lay there like the spilled Seven-Up.

"You look a little peaked, pal," Phil said. "If you ask me, you're trying real hard to catch something. And this is the season for it, too."

"Phil's right," Sue chimed in. "You'd better see if your doctor can give you some kind of prescription."

Carol returned with a damp cloth, mopping up the droplets of liquid that clustered on the upholstery. Harry stood up and brushed at his trousers.

"Who's your man?" Phil asked.

"What?" Harry said.

"Your M.D. Is he a good one?"

"He's all right, I guess. We've never really used him for anything outside of a bad cold. But unless he's got a cure for the clumsies, I don't need a doctor."

"I wouldn't be too sure of that," Phil said solemnly. "I heard there's some virus going around that can put you flat on your back for a week."

"It was just an accident," Carol said in a tone that was meant to convey more than mere words.

"Why, sure," Sue said, suddenly reversing her position. "Phil's an alarmist." She reached out and squeezed Harry's hand. "All you need is a good night's sleep. And we're going to leave right now to make sure you get it."

"Don't be silly. You just got here."

"We'll make it another time," Sue said. "After all, we're right next door."

Harry turned to Carol, but she avoided his glance.

"I still think you ought to call your doctor and see if he can give you something," Phil said.

"Carol knows what's best," Sue said, and took her husband's arm. "Good night, all. We'll be talking to you."

Harry wanted to protest, but he saw that it was useless, and in a few moments he was closing the front door behind the Martins.

Carol's presence next to him made him feel oddly self-conscious.

"I'm sorry I ruined the evening," he said.

"Don't worry about it. They're good friends. They understand."

"Apparently quite a bit."

"What do you mean?"

"You tell me. What did you say to Sue while Phil and I were in mixing the drinks?"

"Just that you'd been having headaches."

"That's all?"

Her soft-blue eyes assumed an almost clinical look. "Is there anything else to tell, Harry?"

She wasn't asking a question; she was waiting for an admission, and it made him uncomfortable.

"Forget it. I think I'll go to bed."

She nodded. "I'll clear things up and be in."

"You don't have to come. It's early."

"Not really, she said, looking at him as if he were a perplexing riddle she was determined to solve.

Harry swung his legs under the sheets, set his electric blanket at four, turned out the light, and eased his aching head down onto the pillow. The pain had been building ever since the first flash of the bell tower earlier in the evening. By now it was a steady throb enveloping his entire skull, and as he lay there staring up at the shadowy outline of the ceiling, he began the too-familiar ritual of counting down the minutes until the aspirin would start to take effect.

Aspirin. He'd probably taken more of the stuff in the past few days than he normally took in a whole year. He wished he had something stronger, but that would mean seeing a doctor. That was an inevitable conclusion that he wanted to put off for as long as possible. Though, he had to admit, that day seemed to be approaching very rapidly. Whatever it was that was going on inside of him was progressing at a frightening pace.

His eyelids grew heavy, and he gave up the effort to keep them open. He was tired, more tired than he'd realized, yet it was barely nine P.M. He supposed it was the aftereffects of the image flashes; they'd no doubt been a terrific strain on his system. Rest. That was what he needed. If he could only have a decent night's sleep, free from the terror of the nightmare, then maybe he could begin to control this thing. Maybe he could defeat it by sheer force of will.

Somewhere in the closing moments of his wakefulness he thought he heard Carol step softly into the room.

He was running again, and the rumbling noise was keeping pace with him, stride for stride. It was just as before. They were after him, and he was fleeing for his life. Yet, something was out of place. He could feel it in the atmosphere, almost a tangible presence telling him that this time it was going to be different. And it was.

As he ran along, struggling to keep his footing, gasping for breath, he heard it. The bells! On a rise, cresting a hill to his left and far in front of him, stood the hazy form of the bell tower. He felt hope—the unreasonable hope of the dying. If it were a church, it would mean sanctuary. Safety. A chance to think, to rack his brain until he found the answer that would tell him why he was being pursued.

He altered his course to bring himself in line with the hill. He felt a renewed vigor as he pushed his body harder than he ever had before. Because now he had a goal. Now he had something to run *to* instead of just something to run *from.* At last there was a genuine chance of escape, no matter how high the odds.

Then he was down. Tripped up again by the same jagged rock. As before, his left leg became a tool of the enemy, transformed by the fall into another instrument of his torture. Once again he dug his hands into the ground and began to crawl, the sound of the bells growing louder with each painful movement.

Suddenly a spray of mist struck his face. He raised his head and saw the elaborate fountain, its colored jets of water dancing nimbly before him. He stopped his agonizing progress, shut his eyes to the graceful geysers of water, and rolled over on his back, awaiting his death. How could he hope to triumph in this fun-house world into which he'd been plunged? Better to let them take him and make an end of it. He steeled himself for the finish.

Nothing.

Slowly, tentatively, he opened his eyes. He knew what he would see—the faceless figures standing over him.

But they weren't there.

Instead, peering back at him with a garish intensity, and distorted to a grotesque size, was the bank of numbered lights with the number twenty-two glowing a bright, eye-piercing red.

He started to laugh, a hysterical cackle that rasped at his throat as it came out, until he thought the noise of his own laughter would kill him. Then it was eclipsed by another sound; the sharp, high-pitched screech knifed through the air, driving a skewer of pain through his ears.

Harry awoke screaming, and jolted upright in bed, his face bathed in a cold, clammy sweat.

5

Carol snapped on the light, the sudden burst of brightness forcing Harry to shut his eyes. When he opened them again, Carol was sitting up in bed next to him regarding him with that same clinical look she'd used earlier in the evening—waiting for him to confess.

"Sorry," he muttered as he dabbed at his sweaty face with a handkerchief. "Just a bad dream."

"I think it's about time you stopped trying to kid me, Harry."

"I'm not kidding anybody. I had a nightmare."

"Of course you did. But there's more to it than that. And I'm your wife. I have a right to know."

He looked at her firm, impassive face and saw there was no point in continuing his muddled attempts at deception. He'd deceived no one, not even himself.

"Let's get some coffee," he said, "and talk."

They put on their robes, and he followed her down the hallway.

In the kitchen he studied the design of the wallpaper as she set out cups and saucers and the large jar of instant coffee. Neither of them had spoken since leaving the bedroom. Then there was the *whoosh* of the gas jet igniting under the teakettle, and Carol pulled up a chair and settled herself across from him at the butcher-block table.

Her face was softer now, ready to absorb his words, and yet, as he sat and looked at her, he couldn't dispel the nagging doubt that everything he was about to tell her, she somehow already knew. Still, that was impossible. She'd been with him for almost ten years, but there had been almost thirty years before that during which she hadn't even known of his existence. She had no special window into his mind.

"I suppose," he said, "I'd better start by apologizing for trying to hide anything from you in the first place."

She smiled. "No apologies necessary. I probably would have done the same thing myself. But that's over now, so just begin at the beginning and tell me everything that's been happening."

Harry sighed and collected his thoughts. Talking to his wife had suddenly become one of the most difficult ordeals of his life. Nevertheless, it had to be done; she was waiting.

"It started with the dream. That was . . . I don't know, four days ago, I guess."

He paused, but she remained silent, prodding him to continue.

"The first time, I didn't think anything of it. Then it came back again the next night, exactly the same dream. And each time, after I'd wake up, I couldn't shake the feeling that I'd never really left the scene of the nightmare. I'd lie there an hour or more, reliving every moment in vivid detail, like there was a loop of movie film in my mind repeating itself over and over."

"Tell me about the dream," she said.

He explained it all as thoroughly as he possibly could. When he got to the end and began describing the high-pitched screech that always jolted him awake, the whistling steam from the teakettle made him start, as if a portion of the nightmare had suddenly invaded the brightly lit cheerfulness of their kitchen.

"Turn it off," he said quickly.

Carol walked over to the cook-top and shut off the gas. The whistle immediately faded away. She brought the steaming kettle to the table and set it on a thickly crocheted hot pad. In silence they each spooned out some instant coffee; then she lifted the kettle over his cup and poured. He watched as the scalding-hot water struck the crystals and immediately took on a dark, rich coloring. As she moved the kettle to repeat the process for herself, the sloshing water caused several quick, excited whistles to escape in little bursts of steam.

He stirred in his usual two spoonfuls of sugar while she sat back down in her chair.

"Now, what about the headaches?" She continued as if she'd never left the table. "When did they start?"

"Yesterday."

"Not before?"

"No. That was the first one. Why?"

She shook her head. "No reason. I just want to get the sequence of events straight."

He had to say it. He had to come right out and ask her; though it was ridiculous and absurd, he had to bring the question out into the open for his own peace of mind. But he was afraid. As a stall, he took a sip of the coffee before he spoke.

"Carol?"

"Yes?"

"Do you know something? About what's going on, I mean?"

"Only what you're telling me."

"Are you sure? Because if you're trying to spare my feelings, there's no point to it. Half the agony I'm going through is because I don't know what the hell's happening to me."

"Listen to me, Harry. I have no secrets from you. I've known for days that something's wrong, because I'm your wife and I've lived with you for almost ten years. And now I want to try to help you fight this thing. All right?"

"I'm sorry. I thought maybe you could see something." Harry paused. "I guess I was just looking for an easy answer."

"Maybe there is one; maybe there isn't. We won't know until we've seen it through and come out the other end. Together."

"I'm beginning to think the other end may very well be disaster."

"Don't talk that way. You've had headaches and a recurring nightmare. I don't think those are particularly unusual symptoms. There could be any number of explanations."

"There's something else," he said softly.

"Tell me."

He hesitated, stirring his coffee.

"Please," she said. "I have to know."

He looked at her for a long moment before he began. "This evening, just before I left the office, something happened to me that . . . that leads me to believe I may be losing my mind."

Ashamed and afraid, he'd spoken the sentence to the tabletop, but now that the words were out, he felt relieved, as if the possibility of hope were not entirely removed from reality. And when his eyes lifted to meet his wife's, he didn't see the pity and shock that he'd expected. What he saw instead was a serene understanding that made him suddenly realize how totally helpless he was without her.

"I want to hear about it," she said. "All of it."

He struggled in his description of that first image flash. Recounting the bizarre bank of numbered lights with its glowing twenty-two that had appeared while he stood at the office water cooler was anything but easy.

When he was finished, Carol remained silent, carefully assessing everything he'd said, and although she had registered surprise during his explanation, she'd never let her expression deteriorate into one of humiliating condescension.

"Do you have any idea what those lights represented?"

"None whatsoever," he replied without any hesitation. "I've tried, but I can't make any sense out of them at all."

"Have you seen the image more than once?"

"Yes. Along with the others." This time he thought he noticed a slight trace of alarm in her eyes.

"There've been others?"

He nodded and described the bells in the tower and the elaborate fountain, trying hard to be as accurate as he could, in the hope that she'd seize on some thread of a rational explanation.

Again she remained thoughtful for a few moments before she spoke.

"When you saw that fountain," she asked, "was there anything in the background that was familiar to you?"

"No, nothing." Why these curious questions? What did she hope to discover?

She answered him quickly, as if anticipating his thoughts. "I was just trying to think if it might have been part of some landmark around here, but I don't ever remember seeing a fountain like that."

"No, we're too rural. It's more like something you'd find in a larger city. Washington, maybe."

Carol shrugged noncommittally. "Dreams are funny things. They can conjure up an image out of disconnected bits and pieces."

"But we could try," he said.

"What do you mean?"

"I mean, drive into D.C. over the weekend and try to find the damn thing."

For the first time, her tone became slightly patronizing. "Honey, we lived in Washington for over nine years. Do you recall ever seeing that fountain while we were there?"

"No." He sighed.

"Neither do I."

"But look," he persisted, "that doesn't necessarily prove anything. People can live in a city all their lives and never get to see half the things that are there."

"All right. And what if we found it—and the bell tower, too? Does it really make any difference where they are? The problem isn't whether or not those things exist; the problem is why they're taking over your mind. That's what we've got to find out."

Harry's glance returned to the tabletop. She was right. The point was, he was *seeing* things. Whether they were little green men or clanging bells in a tower was totally irrelevant. Normal people saw only what was there, and he could no longer classify himself in that category.

Weary, he raised his head and looked at his wife. Though her face was calm, he knew what she was thinking. He also knew that if he was to have half a chance to win this mysterious battle he'd been plunged into, it was up to him to translate her thoughts into words.

Even as he spoke them, he couldn't quite believe that his life had come to this.

"I'm sick, Carol. I need help."

6

The drive to Dr. Simmons' office was lonely. Carol had wanted to come along, but Harry had been firm about her staying home; he didn't want to share his embarrassment with anyone. Now, as he waited at the intersection for the signal to change, he wished he'd taken her up on her offer. The inside of the car seemed a vast expanse in which he was an insignificant little dot. If people happened casually to glance his way, he couldn't suppress the rush of anger that overwhelmed him, and he'd have to fight to tell himself that they were strangers who had never seen him before and would never see him again. He felt as if the entire world knew where he was going and why.

The impatient honk of a horn made him notice that the light was green, and he lurched the car forward with a quick burst of speed while cursing the motorist behind him. Soon, multistory buildings flanked him on the right and left, and he began watching for the address: 1754. It proved to be a sleek black structure with darkly tinted windows that gave it a solemn, brooding appearance. Reluctantly he turned the car into the subterranean parking area and pulled to a stop next to a small, glass-enclosed booth that housed the attendant.

The man tore the perforated ticket in two, tucked one section of it under the left-hand windshield wiper, and gave the other half to Harry.

"Anywhere on level two or three," he said.

Harry pocketed the ticket stub and eased the car down the steep incline of the concrete ramp. As he rounded a curve, the tires squealed on the slick surface and echoed throughout the man-made cavern.

He found a spot on the second level, and when he stepped out of the car, the stench of exhaust filled his nostrils. He turned the key in the lock and looked around to get his bearings. Off to his left he saw a sign marked ELEVATORS.

Jamming his index finger against the up button, he waited impatiently for the doors to open. Once he was inside, he pressed the button for the seventh floor and felt the thrust of the upward motion register slightly in his stomach. He was alone in the elevator, and his eyes wandered aimlessly about the small cubicle.

Then it hit him.

He was looking at the bank of lights that flashed on and off, signaling the various floors that were being passed—*a bank of lights similar to the one he'd seen in the image flash!*

A bell sounded and the doors slid open, admitting him to the seventh floor. Harry stepped slowly out into the corridor and turned to watch the doors move silently together, still mesmerized by the unexpected touch of reality that had rubbed up against his nightmare world.

As he stood there in the hallway, the questions tumbled through his mind at a breakneck pace. Was what he had just seen the hint of a clue, or mere coincidence? Was he trying to force a rational explanation where none would fit? And if the illuminated number twenty-two that had been haunting him was in fact part of an elevator panel, where in the world had it come from? Because, as far as he could remember, he had never had any occasion to go to the twenty-second floor of a building.

Suddenly he became aware of a soft jingling sound in the background. Approaching him from his right was an immensely overweight woman, her bulk draped in a garish floral-print muu-muu and her left wrist encircled by a silver charm bracelet whose tokens clinked together as she walked. Not wanting to be forced into even a casual hello, Harry immediately moved to the office directory that hung on the wall behind him and searched the alphabetical listings until he came to the one he was looking for: Simmons, Richard H., M.D., Internal Medicine. His eyes traveled horizontally across the directory and read Suite 706; then he moved off down the corridor, still puzzled as to whether or not he'd stumbled onto a possible solution to his problem.

He pushed open the door to the reception room and was grateful to see that there was only one other person inside—a young woman who sat reading a copy of *McCall's* and glanced up briefly as he entered. All during the drive over, he'd been dreading the possibility of having to sit in a waiting room full of people.

Harry walked up to the nurse who sat at a desk on the other side of the pass-through that is a fixture in all medical and dental offices.

She interrupted her typing and smiled up at him. "May I help you?"

"My name is Harry Milford. I have a ten-thirty appointment with Dr. Simmons."

"Oh, yes, Mr. Milford. You're a new patient, aren't you?"

"You could say that. I've spoken to the doctor once or twice on the phone but I've never been in to see him."

"Okay. Just have a seat and fill this out." She handed him a large form crammed with printing and attached to a clipboard. "Do you need a pen?"

"No, thanks. I have one."

As he made his way back to a chair, the nurse called to the young woman reading the magazine, "You can come in now, Mrs. Wagner." The woman set the magazine down on the sofa, picked up her purse, and disappeared through a door that stood at a right angle to the pass-through, leaving Harry alone in the waiting room.

He gave a sigh of relief at his privacy and turned his attention to the form in his lap. It was so chock-full of questions that he chuckled to himself, thinking that some former government employee must have designed it. Aside from the usual ritual of name, age, date of birth, and so on, it went into such minute areas as "What medications are you currently taking? Do you have frequent urination and/or accompanying pain? Do you tire easily? Are you prone to shortness of breath? Do you have any known allergies?" The list was seemingly endless, and by the time he'd completed it, Harry felt just the least bit annoyed that his health, or lack of it, had been reduced to seventy-five questions on a form that was probably run off by the thousands in some grimy printing shop by a bored worker.

He walked back to the nurse and handed the clipboard to her. "I answered the questions as best I could."

"Fine. The doctor will see you in just a few minutes."

On the way back to his chair, he picked up the issue of *McCall's* that the young woman had been reading when he came in. Settling himself into the seat, he was struck by something odd about the cover of the magazine. The logo was spelled out in the usual large red letters, below which was the beautiful face of a fashion model. For a moment he was drawn to the picture by an urgent sense of familiarity. Then the feeling left, and he shrugged it off. Surely he had never met that face before.

He opened the magazine at random, and as he sat there staring blankly at the page in front of him, his mind began to anticipate his meeting with Dr. Simmons. Most certainly the doctor would want to discuss Harry's symptoms with him. That would be hard. Harry tried to convince himself that the man was used to hearing all sorts of complaints from all sorts of people, but it did little to ease his apprehension. Of course, if the doctor thought there was evidence of a tumor, that would lay the cause on a completely physical foundation and make things a hell of a lot easier. Immediately Harry chided himself for his macabre thought. Nobody *wants* to have a brain tumor. It was just that he was anxious to have a name pinned to whatever was wrong with him; then, he reasoned, he could begin to cope with it.

"Mr. Milford?" The nurse's voice startled him, and he

looked up abruptly. "You can come in now," she said, and left her desk to open the door for him.

"Right this way," she said as he followed her down a short hallway. Off to his left he glimpsed an open door that revealed Dr. Simmons' private office, but it was empty. Then the nurse stopped in front of an examining room and gestured for him to go inside.

"Remove all your clothes except for your shorts. If you get chilly, you can put on the white gown. The doctor will be right in." At the end of her routine speech she closed the accordionlike partition that sealed off the room.

Harry began to unbutton his shirt and take in his surroundings. The room was small and efficient in size. Directly behind him stood the padded examination table with its strip of clean white paper running down the middle. At a right angle to the table was a counter that extended the entire width of the narrow room and contained an array of bottles and utensils. Against the wall flanking the counter stood an upright scale, and in the corner diagonally opposite the padded table was a small white-porcelain sink with a green bottle of surgical soap resting next to the cold-water tap. A lone chair occupied the small space of wall next to the sink. The hospital gown was neatly folded across it.

He had just finished placing his slacks over one of the wire hangers that dangled from a hook next to the doorway when the partition slid open and Dr. Simmons entered the room.

"Mr. Milford, I'm Richard Simmons. Glad to know you." He grasped Harry's right hand in a firm handshake and then set down the file folder that he'd carried in with him. "Just let me scrub up, and I'll be right with you. Have a seat on the table."

As Harry hoisted himself up onto the examination table, he observed Dr. Simmons. A young man of perhaps thirty-seven or thirty-eight, he stood about five feet ten and weighed in at around one seventy-five, the ten or twelve pounds he could stand to lose concentrated in his midsection, which bulged slightly beneath the white lab coat. He had a few strands of premature gray in his sideburns, and when he turned toward Harry, he flashed a smile that hinted at compassion beyond his years.

He opened the file folder and studied the form Harry had filled out in the waiting room.

"It says here you're allergic to penicillin. When did you discover that?"

"When I was a child. I had a sinus infection and was running a fever. The doctor prescribed it in some capsules, and that night I broke out in a rash from head to foot. Of course, if you thought it was necessary, I suppose I could always put up with a rash for a couple of days."

"The rash was a warning, Mr. Milford. If your system were to assimilate penicillin a second time, the results could very likely be a lot more serious. But don't worry; if the need ever arises, there are always other drugs we can substitute."

With that, Dr. Simmons began the examination, listening to the heart and lungs; recording weight, blood pressure, and pulse; checking for hernia and any telltale signs of prostate difficulties; shining lights up his nose, down his throat, and into his ears; rapping his knees and elbows with the rubber-tipped hammer.

"Now, Mr. Milford, sit up and close your eyes." Harry did as he was told.

"What I'm going to do," the doctor continued, "is trace two numbers on the palm of each hand. When I'm finished, I want you to tell me what numbers I traced, and on which hand. All right?"

"Sure. Go ahead."

Dr. Simmons traced the numerals with a retracted ballpoint pen. "You can open your eyes now. What did I write?"

"You drew three and five on the right hand, eight and six on the left."

The doctor made a notation on the chart.

"How'd I do?" Harry asked.

"Perfect. Now I'm going to turn you over to Miss Warren

for blood and urine samples and an EKG. Then you can get dressed, and I'll see you in my office."

About twenty minutes later he entered the doctor's private office. It was a comfortably furnished room done in browns and golds. Simmons occupied a high-backed leather chair behind the desk and motioned for Harry to have a seat on the sofa.

"Well, Mr. Milford, we won't have the blood and urine results until tomorrow, but your EKG checked out just fine. In fact, the only abnormality I was able to detect was in your blood pressure; it's moderately high. Have you been under any particular stress lately other than from the headaches and nightmares you mentioned over the phone?"

"You mean all I have is high blood pressure?" Harry asked, deliberately avoiding the doctor's question.

"Why? What did you think it might be?" His tone was sincere, trying to root out his patient's anxiety.

"Oh, nothing, really."

"If you didn't think anything was wrong, you wouldn't have pressed me for an appointment today. Please, I'd like to know what was on your mind."

"It sounds pretty silly now, but I thought I had a brain tumor."

Dr. Simmons leaned back in his chair and clasped his hands together on the desk. "I know you did. Your wife called me after you left the house this morning and expressed that fear to me. She also told me about the image flashes. I was hoping you would give me that information yourself. It's nothing to be ashamed of, you know."

Harry felt the blood rush to his cheeks. "All right, doctor, I was wrong. I should have told you. But when you said all I had was high blood pressure . . . well, that leaves only one alternative, doesn't it?"

"Really? What's that?"

"You know as well as I do."

"No, I don't. Tell me."

He was angry now, and he looked Simmons square in the eye when he spoke.

"If a tumor isn't causing my problems, then I must be losing my mind. Is that what you wanted to hear?"

"No. But you did."

"Oh, come on! What are you trying to do, tell me I want to go insane?"

"What I'm trying to tell you, Mr. Milford, is that you're jumping to conclusions. I'm not a psychiatrist, and this is the first time I've met you, but I will say this: there are a lot more avenues we have to exhaust before I'll consider that mental illness may be the cause of your problems. However, if we're going to make any progress, you'll have to be open and above board with me. That means *you're* going to have to tell me your symptoms, not your wife."

Harry controlled his emotions before he spoke. "Okay. But if it isn't a tumor, then what is it?"

"I never ruled out the tumor, Mr. Milford. And I don't say that to frighten you. But there's only so much we can determine in an office exam. So I'd like to put you in the hospital for further tests."

"Look, doctor, I appreciate what you're trying to do for me. Really. But I'll be honest with you. I don't like hospitals. I never have. And so far today I haven't had any problems. So I'd like to give this thing a little more time to go away by itself."

"How much time did you have in mind?"

"A week. If I haven't made any solid progress in a week, then you can put me in the hospital. All right?"

Simmons smiled. "Do I have a choice?"

"No. I'm afraid not."

The doctor nodded and reached for his prescription pad.

"These are some pills to control your blood pressure. I want you to take one every morning before breakfast. And if any new symptoms occur, get on the phone to me right away. I don't care what time it is. Understand?"

"I understand." Harry almost told him about the possible clue he'd discovered in the elevator, but he was afraid of sounding foolish.

He stood up and took the prescription from Simmons, trying to read the illegible scrawl.

"One of these days you guys are going to learn how to write."

"No way. Lousy penmanship is a prerequisite for medical school."

The two men shook hands.

"Remember," Simmons said, "no more cereal-box diagnoses. Let me be the doctor."

"I'll remember," Harry said, and turned to leave.

"Oh, one more thing," Simmons called after him. "Where did you get that scar?"

"Scar?" Harry asked, turning back toward the doctor.

"On your left ankle. I noticed it while I was examining you. You didn't mention anything about it on your form, and I like to keep my records complete."

"Oh, that. I fell out of a tree when I was a kid and broke my ankle. The bone came right through the skin."

"How old were you?"

"I don't know. Ten, eleven maybe."

Simmons hesitated before he answered. "Okay. I'll make a note of it."

"Right. And thanks for everything. I'll be in touch."

By the time he reached his car, Harry's mind was whirling. He unlocked the door and sat sideways on the front seat, his feet resting outside on the white line that delineated the parking space. Quickly he unlaced his left shoe and removed the sock. Then he raised his foot and began to examine the area of his ankle. Soon he found what he was looking for. There, on the inside of his leg, amid the black hairs that covered his anklebone, was the thin white line of a scar no more than an inch long.

His mouth went dry. There had been no childhood fall from a tree, despite his glib explanation to Simmons. He had never had a scar on his body at any time in his life. But there was one there now—in the exact spot where his left foot always slammed into the jagged rock in his nightmare.

7

By the time he arrived at the Maryland agency, he was still numb from the discovery he'd made. As he entered the spacious lobby, the security guard gave him a friendly wave, and Harry managed to utter a few vacant words of acknowledgment.

Once he was seated behind his desk, surrounded by the welcome shield of the green partitions, he immediately picked up the phone and started to dial his home number. Halfway through, he stopped and returned the receiver to its cradle. He'd been ready to tell Carol all about the scar and the panel of lights in the elevator, but suddenly he was filled with indecision.

Angry with his response, he sought the reason behind it. Was it because he didn't trust her? That was absurd, he told himself. She'd never given him any cause to doubt her. After all, he reasoned, hadn't she been the one who'd sat and listened to his bizarre recitation just last night—without the slightest trace of condescension? Certainly his story must have sounded strange to her, at the very least. Yet he was sure she'd believed every word he'd told her. She'd even tried to help him sort it all out, but of course she couldn't; for that matter, neither could he. Until today, because now he had something real, something he could reach out and touch. True, the elevator panel was still somewhat of a theory, but at least it fit; it made sense. And the scar was something that couldn't be denied.

Then a sickening thought struck him: What if he had some

kind of progressive amnesia? What if the memories of his life were slowly washing away like so much silt from the banks of a river? He felt his stomach knot as the hope drained from his body.

"No, damnit," he said aloud, "it can't be." He forced himself to comb the events of his personal history, but try as he might, he couldn't conjure up even the slightest remembrance of an accident that had left a scar on his ankle or anywhere else.

Suddenly it occurred to him that there was a way he could verify his position. He picked up the phone and dialed extension 311, drumming his fingers nervously on the gray metal desk as he waited for an answer.

"Hello?" said a man's voice at the other end. "Wallace speaking."

"Harry Milford, Frank. I need a favor."

"Sure. What can I do for you?"

"I want to take a look at the dossier of one of the people in my section."

"That's easy enough. Whose?"

"Mine."

"Yours? What the hell for?"

He swore silently for not having thought up an excuse ahead of time. "I can't explain right now. But I need it. Can you pull the strip for me? I'll be right up."

"Okay, Harry. Whatever you say."

"And, Frank, do it yourself, will you? I'd like to keep this just between the two of us."

"Consider it done."

"Thanks. I really appreciate it."

Harry hung up the phone and weighed the possibility of whether or not Frank would respect the confidence of his unusual request. Not that there'd be any particular problem if the word got out; as a supervisor, Harry had access to the files of anyone in his section. But there was no getting away from the fact that his wanting to look at his own dossier would certainly seem a little odd. Nevertheless, he felt that his secret was safe, and he couldn't help smiling at the reason why.

About three months ago a new boy in the mail room had gotten the interoffice-correspondence pouches mixed up. The pouch for each section was identified by a color-coded triangle in the upper-left-hand corner. Harry's section was red; Frank's was green. But they'd gotten reversed one morning, and Harry had broken the seal and removed the contents before he realized it wasn't his. Though classified material was never distributed in this fashion, if any of the supervisors wanted to pass on some juicy bits of gossip, they'd write the memo in a simple binary code that none of the lower-level personnel knew. On the top of the stack that morning was a coded message from one of the more attractive women in the agency thanking Frank for a wonderful time the previous night and asking when they could do it again. Which was fine, except for the fact that Frank Wallace was a very married man, and when he'd rushed into Harry's office to exchange pouches, it had become obvious—though nothing was actually said—that his indiscretion had been discovered.

Harry sat alone in one of the small individual viewing rooms that lined a wall of the document section. Quickly he turned the black knob that fed the strip of microfilm through the viewer, skipping over the bulk of the information contained in his file until he came to the heading he was looking for: Medical History. He slowed his pace as he scanned the data carefully; then he stopped the strip cold and blinked once at the words that stared back at him. He repeated them over and over in his mind, unconsciously forming their jubilant message with his lips. Identifying Marks: None.

So the confusion was not all in his mind!

When he returned to his office, he was faced with the decision of whether or not to call Carol and tell her his discovery. He wanted to trust her completely. Why didn't he? It was just a feeling, something he couldn't put a name to, and the more he tried to the angrier he became with himself.

Then the phone rang.

"Hello?"

"This is Jean, Mr. Milford. Mr. Hastings would like to see you in his office. Right away."

"Sounds important."

"I don't know. But he's expecting you."

"Tell him I'm on my way."

Peter Hastings was the head of the Maryland agency, and as such, he reported directly to someone in Washington, D.C.—a someone whose name only five other individuals in the agency knew.

Harry had been formally introduced to Hastings the first day he'd reported to work, some six months ago. At the time, he'd found his new boss to be exactly what he'd come to expect—a polite middle-aged individual with a nondescript face and a personality that was altogether forgettable. The government didn't like people who stood out in a crowd to occupy potentially volatile positions.

This was to be his first personal contact with Hastings since that initial meeting, the interim having been punctuated with occasional interoffice memos and a random bulletin or two.

Harry pushed open the door and entered the outer office.

Jean immediately acknowledged him. "Hello, Mr. Milford. You can go right in."

"Thanks," he said, but she was no longer looking at him, having already returned her attention to the paperwork on her desk.

Inside his office, Hastings stood up as Harry came in, a gesture that struck him as rather out of place. Then they shook hands and seated themselves opposite each other.

"Cigarette?" Hastings asked as he lifted the top of an inlaid-teak humidor.

"No, thanks, I don't smoke."

"Good for you. I quit once, for two years. Then one day everything went wrong from beginning to end, and I was hooked again."

"That can happen," Harry said, and felt uncomfortable. He wasn't used to trading small talk with people on Hastings' level.

"Tell me, do you feel you're getting along well here at the agency? You were with us for several years in Washington. It must have been difficult for you and your wife to pull up stakes and adjust to a new environment after all that time."

"I always knew the day might come when I'd have to move. And so did Carol. As for my work here, I'm very happy. Have there been any complaints?"

"No, no, of course not. I certainly didn't mean to imply that we were dissatisfied with you. Far from it. In fact, if anything, we've been most impressed with your performance. Your output has been concise and extremely relevant. That's why we feel you've earned a little vacation."

The words hung in the air for a brief interval before Harry fully absorbed them.

"Vacation? But I'm not due until—"

"Nonsense," Hastings cut in. "Take a couple of weeks off and relax. I understand you and Carol have an anniversary coming up. Consider this an early celebration. Get away somewhere, just the two of you. You deserve it."

"It really isn't necessary, Mr. Hastings."

"Believe me, Harry, it is." His tone was pleasant, but it left no doubt that the conversation was over.

"What can I say?" he replied, and could hear the strain in his voice.

"You don't have to say anything. Just enjoy yourself. Beginning now."

Hastings stood up and extended his hand. As their two palms clasped, Harry tried to read some sign of explanation in the other man's face, but all he saw was calm indifference.

"Shit," Harry said as soon as he'd stepped into the hall and closed the door to Jean's outer office behind him.

Although he had no choice but to accept his enforced "vacation," that didn't prevent the anger from steadily mounting inside him as he drove home.

It just didn't add up. The fact that he'd taken a couple of hours off for a physical certainly shouldn't have prompted that kind of reaction from Hastings. Of course, Hastings hadn't mentioned anything about Harry's visit to the doctor, but that had to be the real reason behind his decision. Could Hastings have gotten Simmons to break the confidentiality of the doctor-patient relationship and thus found out about the headaches and the image flashes? That was a possibility, but not a very probable one, Harry decided. Simmons hadn't struck him as the type who ran scared at the mention of a government title. Besides, the only verifiable symptom he could report would be high blood pressure, and even that could be kept under control with medication.

No, Simmons wasn't the one who'd blown the whistle on him.

What about Frank Wallace? That didn't fit either. So what if he'd asked Frank to see his own personnel file? Maybe the request was a little unusual, but that was the worst that could be said for it. And Frank would be foolish to jeopardize Harry's trust unless he wanted to run the risk of his own dirty linen being aired in public. So that quickly scratched him from the list of possible informers, leaving only one.

Carol.

The conclusion settled in his chest like a mass of wet cement. He didn't want to believe it, yet his mind was void of any rationalizations that could absolve her of guilt. The fact that her actions would have been well-intentioned did little to excuse the damage she had done.

He was so full of frustration and anger that he almost missed the turn onto his street and had to brake hard to make it, the tires screeching in protest. He came to a sharp stop in the driveway, slammed the gearshift into park, and switched off the ignition. Then he sat there for a few moments and tried to calm himself. Barging into the house and starting an argument wasn't going to solve anything. If Carol had been responsible, he'd know soon enough.

Harry unlocked the front door and heard his wife's voice from the den; she was talking on the telephone.

"I think Harry's just come home, Sue. I'll talk to you later."

He walked into the den as she was hanging up the phone.

"What's the matter?" she asked, her voice full of concern. "I thought you were going into the office after your physical?"

"I did."

"Then why are you home so early?"

"Don't you know?"

Carol bristled at the injustice. "Of course I don't. Now, tell me what's happened."

"Hastings has ordered me to take a two-week vacation." He spoke the words in a flat monotone, his displeasure clearly evident.

"But why? Was it Dr. Simmons' idea?"

"Simmons found nothing more than a little high blood pressure. Besides, Hastings never even mentioned the doctor; he didn't have to. It's obvious they feel I may no longer be reliable, and they're buying themselves some time to think over their options. 'An early anniversary celebration,' Hastings called it. Bullshit."

"I just don't understand it," she said.

"I think you do."

"What do you mean?"

"Look, Carol, there's no sense in beating around the bush. Did you call Hastings and tell him what's been happening to me?" He hated the sound of the question as soon as he'd spoken it.

She was hurt and bewildered. "How in the world would I ever get through to Hastings?"

"You tell me. You called up Dr. Simmons because you didn't trust me to tell him everything that was going on."

"And would you have?"

"Yes. . . I don't know. But that's not what I asked you. Did you talk to Hastings?"

"No!"

"Well, somebody did, damnit! And how the hell else would he know that we had an anniversary coming up?"

"Maybe he looked it up in the files."

"He's got better things to do than that."

"And you've got better things to do than to stand here and accuse me! Do you want to check and see if the house is bugged? For Christ's sake, Harry, stop being paranoid!"

The word was a stinging slap in the face, and they both felt ashamed of their behavior.

"I'm sorry," she said. "I didn't mean that."

"Forget it. You could be right. I'm the one who should be apologizing. Forgive me?"

They embraced, and she rested her head on his shoulder. "Maybe it's all for the best."

"I suppose," he said. "Anyway, I don't have a choice. But I'm still convinced that Hastings knows what's been going on. I just wish I knew how."

Carol looked up into his face. "You work for the government, and you have a lot of responsibility. Don't beat your head against a stone wall. It's part of their job to find things out about people. You know that."

"Sure—all part of their job. And they do it very well."

"You've got two weeks to rest and unwind. We could go somewhere; a change of scenery would do us both good. And maybe you'll find the answers you've been looking for."

Suddenly he was exhausted, his eyelids an unbearably heavy burden. "Right now, what I need is a little nap. Do you mind?"

"Of course not. Go in the bedroom and close the drapes. I was going to do some vacuuming, but it can wait."

"Thanks." He gave her a quick kiss and left the room.

Harry was standing alone at the bedroom window, just ready to close the drapes, when he saw the Martins' car pull into their driveway next door. A moment later, Sue struggled out of the front seat with a bag of groceries under each arm. At first, the implication of what he was seeing didn't register. Then he recalled what Carol had said when she'd hung up the phone after he got home.

She had been talking to Sue. At least, that was the impression she'd given. But it was a lie. Sue couldn't have possibly gotten to the grocery store and back in the short space of his and Carol's conversation.

Who had Carol been talking to? And why had she lied to keep it from him?

Harry pulled the drapes shut and walked over to the bed. As he lay down, a new image flashed before his eyes—another piece of that damnable puzzle that had come from nowhere to stalk his life like an alien shadow. The image was of two computer-tape reels. They were spinning wildly—stopping, starting, and reversing their course in a seemingly random pattern of movement. Then they were gone.

The exhaustion took full control of him, and he closed his eyes, waiting for the dream he knew would come.

8

"Hey." The voice called down to him through layers of restless sleep. "Hey," it repeated again, "wake up. Don't you want any dinner?"

Carol stood beside the bed as Harry came awake. The room was dark, and it took him a few seconds to realize where he was. Then he remembered the swift succession of events that had filled the morning hours, and suddenly he felt uncomfortable in the presence of his wife.

"That was some little nap you took," she said. "It's after six. I didn't have the heart to wake you for lunch. You must be starved."

He wasn't the slightest bit hungry. The only thing he wanted was the information that she was withholding from him. He raised himself up on his elbow, and a jolt of pain passed through his head.

"Headache?" she asked.

"Yeah. I'm just going to stay in bed. Okay?"

"Sure. I'll fix your dinner on a tray."

"No. Just some aspirin. I really don't feel like eating anything."

"But I think it might help."

"I can't, Carol. I just want to sleep. It's been a lousy day."

"All right. I'll get you your aspirin," she said, and walked out of the room.

When she was gone, Harry lay back down and considered confronting her with her lie about the telephone call, but he quickly dismissed the thought. What was to stop her from telling another lie in its place?

Soon she was back with the pills and a glass of water. "You should have asked Dr. Simmons to give you something stronger for the pain."

"I'll call him tomorrow."

He set the glass down on the nightstand. Then she took his pajamas from the closet and laid them on the foot of the bed.

"You'd better change right away, before you fall asleep."

"I will," he said.

Carol reached down and took his hand, like a mother comforting a sick child. "Sleep well. If you need anything, just call."

"Thanks."

Alone in the room, Harry felt as if he were in exile in his own home. He could trust no one, and for a moment a suffocating feeling of helplessness took hold of him. He fought it off, threw back the covers, and got out of bed. He clicked on the light, and as he changed into his pajamas, he began mentally to prepare himself for his solitary struggle against an unknown enemy. The more he thought about it, the angrier he became. He didn't give a damn what the odds were; he wasn't going to let his life be yanked out from under him. Somehow, someway, he was going to find out what the hell was going on. Then he could begin to live again.

Sitting down on the edge of the bed, he raised his left foot and looked again at the small scar on the inside of his ankle. Thoughtfully, he traced its outline back and forth with his finger. "You had to come from somewhere," he said softly, knowing that when he learned the secret of that tiny line he'd be very close to a solution.

Then he switched off the light and drew the covers across his body, anxious for sleep, because he felt certain that within the dark corners of the nightmare rested the keys to his future.

He awoke to the even breathing of Carol beside him in bed. As usual, he felt the quick rhythm of his heart and the stark intensity of fear that were always present after the dream. But this time they were a challenge. Being careful not to wake his wife, he rolled over and peered through the darkness at the green glow of the luminous dial of the clock on his nightstand. It was only a few minutes after eleven, which was good. That meant that Carol would have come to bed only a short time ago and would still be in a deep sleep, not prone to wake and disturb his thoughts.

Harry clasped his hands behind his head and fixed his gaze on the shadowy outline of the light fixture that dangled from the center of the ceiling. He felt exhilarated at the new piece of information that had come to him during the nightmare. Yet there was a doubt to be resolved. Up until now, the other pieces of the puzzle had been sealed in mystery. But this one was directly traceable to a past event, for in the midst of his dream a face had appeared to him—the face of the woman on the cover of the *McCall's* magazine that he'd picked up in Dr. Simmons' waiting room.

He forced the rapid pace of his thoughts to slow, and began methodically adding up the pros and cons of his new discovery. On the one hand, he had to admit that the cover girl might not be connected at all with the other segments of the dream. It could merely be feedback from the tense ordeal of seeing the doctor. But why that particular image? He answered himself quickly, recalling Carol's remark when he'd first explained everything to her that night in the kitchen. "Dreams are funny things," she'd said. "They can conjure up images out of disconnected bits and pieces." Of course, she was right. Science was just beginning to make a dent in the field of dreams. They knew they happened, but they didn't know precisely why, and the cause of the selective processes that governed them was wide open to various explanations, none of which could be empirically verified. So Harry couldn't deny the possibility that he'd dreamed about the woman for the simple reason that she was beautiful.

Still, he felt there was more to it than that. There had been a vivid sense of familiarity when he'd looked at the woman's face. True, the feeling had been a passing one, but it had been there nevertheless, and feelings were all he had to go on at this stage of the game. He couldn't afford not to play a hunch; at least, not one as strong as this.

The woman, he decided, was somehow connected with the other apparitions that were peppering his waking and sleeping hours with their obscure message. He looked at the peaceful form of his wife lying next to him. For close to ten years he had loved her—and still did. Yet, somewhere in his past, or perhaps his future, a relationship with another woman waited to be uncovered.

Carefully he leaned over and brushed Carol's bare shoulder with a kiss. She stirred slightly, and he was saddened by the thought that their life together might never again be the same.

The following morning Harry sat down to breakfast feeling better than he had in days. He had no headache, and though he knew there was still a long way to go before he found the end of the maze, for the first time he was anxious to learn what would be waiting for him there.

Carol set a plate of scrambled eggs and bacon in front of him. "Don't forget your pill," she said.

"Hmm?" he answered, preoccupied with his thoughts.

"Your blood-pressure pill. You're supposed to take it before breakfast. Remember?"

"Oh, sure." He looked down at the table. A small green tablet lay atop the neatly folded napkin that rested beside his fork. He poured himself some orange juice from a plastic pitcher and swallowed the medication. He completed the act swiftly, without thinking, and it wasn't until he bit into the first strip of bacon that it occurred to him that he hadn't the slightest idea of what he'd just taken. His expression reflected the implications of the thought, and Carol looked at him quizzically.

"What's wrong?" she asked. "Did I get the bacon too crisp?"

"No, it's fine. I was just wondering, what's the name of those pills?"

She shrugged. "I don't know. I got the prescription filled

yesterday while you were asleep. They're in the medicine cabinet, if you want to check."

"Thanks."

He made a move to get up, but she stopped him.

"Honey, please; after breakfast. Your eggs'll get cold."

He pulled his chair back in. "Sorry. Just curious, I guess."

The toaster popped up two pieces of bread, and he felt ashamed for even considering the possibility that Carol had given him anything other than the proper medication.

"You certainly should be rested after all the sleep you got."

"I feel good," he said. "And I've decided that I'm going to enjoy my time off. To hell with Hastings." He finished his orange juice and hoped that he'd sounded convincing.

"I'm glad to hear you say that. I think these two weeks are going to do you a world of good."

He took a forkful of eggs and watched as she spread some strawberry preserves on her toast. She seemed calm and relaxed, and he decided that his little act had been well-received.

After breakfast, Carol mentioned that she had some errands to run. "Anything special you want me to pick up while I'm out?"

"Not that I can think of. How long will you be gone?"

"About an hour, an hour and a half." She smiled.

"What's funny?"

"I was just thinking of all the articles I've read about wives who go crazy when their husbands are home during the day."

"I'll do my best to live up to the image."

"I'm sure you will."

A few minutes later, after he'd watched cautiously from the living-room window until her car was out of sight, he went into the den and looked up the number of the telephone company. Before calling, he silently rehearsed the speech he'd devised, then picked up the phone and dialed. He wasn't sure it would work, but it was certainly worth a try.

"Billing department, please," he said to the woman who

answered. There were several clicks as his call was transferred, and for a moment he thought he was going to get cut off.

"Billing, Miss Burns speaking. Can I help you?"

"Yes, Miss Burns. My name is Milford." He spelled it for her. "My problem is a little unusual, but I hope you can give me the information I need. You see, my wife and I have reason to believe that our cleaning woman has been using our phone for long-distance calls, and we'd like to verify it if we can."

"Your monthly bill contains an itemized list of all numbers dialed from your phone, sir."

"I realize that, but we think she just started making the calls over the past six or eight days, and we don't want to have to wait until the next bill comes to find out."

"I see. What is your account number, please?"

"Just a moment. I'll look it up."

Harry set down the receiver and opened the desk drawer where Carol kept the paid bills on file. He quickly riffled through them until he found a recent telephone bill.

"Hello, Miss Burns? The account number is 13576-842-9543."

"And your phone number?"

"Five-five-five, one-four-three-six."

"Hold the line, please."

Harry knew the call Carol had made the preceding day might very well have been local, but if he'd requested a readout of every number called, he probably wouldn't have gotten anywhere. If it wasn't a long-distance number, he was prepared to ask if he could drive over and look at their complete bill up to the present date.

Miss Burns was gone for perhaps two full minutes before she returned. "Mr. Milford?"

"Yes, I'm here." He could feel himself tense while waiting for her response.

"The printout shows only one long-distance call from your phone during the last ten days. And that was yesterday at one-oh-six P.M. to Washington, D.C. The number called was five-five-five, nine-five-eight-one, area code two-oh-two."

He copied the number on a scratch pad.

"Thank you, Miss Burns. You've been a great help."

"You're welcome, sir. Good-bye."

Harry hung up the phone and stared at the number on the small white pad. It meant nothing to him. He spent fifteen minutes scanning their personal directory, but it wasn't in there either. Yet, at the other end of that Washington telephone number was the person to whom Carol had been speaking when he'd arrived home yesterday afternoon.

Nausea mingled with excitement as he started to dial. He didn't know what he was going to say, probably make up some excuse about a wrong number and hope he could get them to identify themselves. If that didn't work, he would try to get someone at the agency to trace it for him, though that would be very risky, considering that he was supposed to be on "vacation."

He listened intently to the rapid series of beeps as the connection went through. Then he heard it ring. He was able to swallow once before there was an answer and a woman's voice began to speak.

"The number you have reached is no longer in service. Please make sure you have dialed correctly before asking for operator assistance. Thank you."

The singsong voice of the recording was halfway through its message for the second time before Harry slammed down the receiver in frustration.

9

Angry at his unexpected setback, Harry picked up the phone and dialed the operator. There was a maddening delay before it was answered.

"Operator."

"Listen," Harry said, "I just dialed area code two-oh-two, five-five-five, nine-five-eight-one, and got a recording saying it was a disconnected number. But there must be some mistake; the number was working yesterday afternoon."

"I'll have to connect you with the Washington operator. One moment, please."

Before he could say anything, he was placed on hold. A few seconds later a new voice came on the line.

"Washington," she said. "May I help you?"

He explained the situation to her.

"I'll check it for you, sir." After a short pause she said, "That number is no longer in service."

"Well, it must have been changed to *something,*" he said impatiently.

"We don't show a new number." She spoke with an irritating cheerfulness, and he wanted to reach through the phone and shake the urgency of the situation into her.

"All right, then just tell me who the number belonged to," he said.

"I'm afraid we can't give out that information."

"Why not? It must be in the Washington phone book."

"I'm sorry, sir. It was an unlisted number."

His stomach burned with anger. He considered asking to speak to a supervisor, but he knew he'd get the same set of routine answers.

"Okay, operator. Thanks anyway."

He hung up and came very close to having the agency track down the source of the phone number for him, but it would almost certainly get back to Hastings, and that could spell the end of everything. Besides, there were other clues to track down. Looking at his watch, he saw that Carol would be gone for at least another forty or forty-five minutes, maybe longer. He hurried into the bedroom, filled his pockets with car keys, money clip, and wallet, and was soon shutting the back door of the house behind him.

He drove directly to a small weathered stucco building located in what had been the main retail section of town until the sprawling new mall sucked all the better merchants into the nearby suburb.

Hand-lettered signs on the front of the dilapidated building proclaimed its purpose: USED BOOKS; WE BUY AND SELL; ADULT BOOKS TOO; COME IN AND BROWSE. Harry pushed open the front door, and the jingle of a little bell announced his presence. The sound triggered a flash of the larger bells ringing in the tower and brought him to a quick stop while he waited for the image to vanish.

The interior of the shop was a marvel of chaos. Stacks of books and magazines all but obliterated the tops of several wooden tables. The entire scene was surrounded by shelves that stretched from floor to ceiling, their cross-members bowed with the weight of the volumes of print that were their burden. As he looked around, Harry could see nothing that resembled any kind of a catalog system, so he approached the only other person in the shop, who he assumed was the owner.

"Excuse me," he said, feeling somehow embarrassed at interrupting the man's reading.

The proprietor lowered a tattered hardback edition from in front of his face and looked out at Harry through steel-rimmed glasses with lenses so thick they made the brown eyes behind them appear as two badly tarnished copper pennies.

"Eh-yeah?" the man grunted in a thick New England accent.

"I'm looking for a back issue of *McCall's*. Do you handle that?"

"If we got it, it'd be over there." He pointed to a particularly large table piled high with magazines. Harry balked at the prospect of plunging into that mountain of paper.

"The issue I want is last month's. Would you have anything that recent?"

"Might. Like I said, if we got it, it's over there."

Harry nodded and walked over to the table, resigned to the task ahead of him. Not knowing where to start, he grabbed a handful of magazines and began sorting through them. There were issues of the *Saturday Evening Post, Life,* and *Look* that were years old, and he found himself wondering if they might someday be collectors' items. He amused himself with the scenario that, buried somewhere in the tons of worthless print that filled the small store was a priceless first edition that held the myopic New Englander's fortune but would go unnoticed until after his death, when the contents of the shop would be appraised for public auction. Then, as he turned over a dog-eared copy to see what it was, the face of the woman was suddenly smiling up at him from the cover. Again the rush of recognition and familiarity swept over him, and again it left him standing alone, looking at a stranger's face and trying desperately to place it in a meaningful context. He fingered the cover of the magazine as if it held some secret braille message. Staring hard into the woman's dark-brown eyes, he forced his mind to tell him who she was and where he had met her, yet all he got in return were several lightning-quick flashes of the wildly spinning computer-tape reels that had first come to greet him yesterday afternoon just after he'd seen Sue Martin pull into her driveway.

He waited until the images left him in peace, then walked back to the proprietor.

"I found what I was looking for. How much do I owe you?"

The old book came down and exposed the copper-penny eyes.

"A dollar-fifty."

"But the magazine costs only seventy-five cents on the newsstands."

"Eh-yeah. 'Cept anybody coulda bought it then."

"All right, I'm not going to argue with you."

"Wouldn't do no good anyhow. I charge what I charge."

Seconds later, as he slid behind the wheel of his car, a thought struck Harry. He opened the magazine, and at the bottom of the contents page was a credit for the cover photo, giving the name of the model: Diane Kinney.

He started the engine and pulled out into traffic. He'd found the name behind the face; his next job was to find the person behind the name.

By the time he arrived home, it was clear to him that he was going to have to approach his investigation in an orderly manner. He had no idea how complex the information might turn out to be, and if he didn't begin taking concise notes now, he could easily find himself mired in a sea of data.

Entering the den, he sat at the desk and in the upper-left-hand corner of a clean white sheet of paper he printed a single word in careful block lettering: PHENOMENA. Then he underscored it and began his list.

PHENOMENA

1. Nightmare
2. Images:
    a) bank of lights with number twenty-two (could be elevator panel)
    b) bells ringing in tower
    c) fountain
    d) computer-tape reels

3. Scar on inside of left ankle
4. Cover girl from *McCall's* (Diane Kinney)

On the opposite side of the paper he printed another heading and began a second, parallel list.

KEY QUESTIONS
1. When did (or will) I meet Diane Kinney?
2. Where did the scar come from?
3. How much does Hastings know?
4. How much does Carol know?

He read and reread the two lists, mentally arranging items from each column in every combination he could think of, hoping each time that the coupling of two of the points might jog some long-forgotten memory. His concentration was so intense that he was only vaguely aware of the sound of the front door opening and closing.

"What in the world are you doing?"

Carol's voice startled him, and he actually jumped a little in his seat.

"Jesus, you scared me. How long have you been standing there?"

"Not long. You didn't even hear me come in. What's all that?" She indicated the paper on the desk.

"It's the beginning of my investigation."

"Your investigation?"

"That's right. I've decided that I'm going to make some sense out of what's been going on."

"And have you?"

"Not yet. But there's plenty of blank paper waiting to be filled up."

"May I see?" she asked.

"Sure." There was nothing he could do to prevent it, so he handed her the two lists.

Harry watched her reactions closely as she stood there

reading his notations. When he saw the frown cross her face, he knew she'd come to the last question.

Carol released the paper a few inches above the desktop, and it landed softly next to Harry's right hand.

"The answer to your fourth question is 'nothing.' " Her voice was cold and tinged with an unmistakable trace of irritation.

"Look, I'm just trying to be thorough, that's all."

"By accusing your own wife?"

"I'm not accusing anybody," he said. "I'm just considering all the possibilities."

"Well, that's one possibility I don't particularly care for. And I shouldn't think you would, either."

"I don't."

"What's that supposed to mean?"

"Nothing."

"Oh, come on, Harry. Maybe you enjoy playing Charlie Chan, but inscrutable you're not."

"All right, you want to know why you're on the list? I'll tell you. Who were you talking to on the telephone when I came home from the agency yesterday?"

She looked genuinely surprised at the question. "Why . . . Sue Martin. I don't understand. What are you getting at?"

"What I'm getting at, Carol, is that it couldn't have been Sue you were talking to, because three or four minutes later, when I went in to lie down, I saw her pull into her driveway and get out of the car with an armload of groceries. So she couldn't have been the one on the other end of the phone."

Harry felt sick at the confrontation. Nothing like this had ever before intruded into their marriage, and he wished he'd never caught his wife in her lie. As he sat there waiting for her answer, he could see the tears beginning to form in her eyes. When she spoke, her voice quivered with the strain of trying to remain calm.

"I guess I'm not very lucky, am I? I mean, what are the odds that you'd ever find out it wasn't Sue?"

"Just tell me," he said softly. "We can't afford to have any secrets."

She nodded and wiped away the trickle of a tear. "I was talking to Dr. Simmons. I thought . . . well, I thought that maybe you hadn't told me everything he'd said. And when you walked in suddenly, I was embarrassed, so I pretended to be talking to Sue. That's it. Except for one thing; I called him because I love you, Harry, and I knew that if he'd given you some bad news, you'd try to keep it from me for as long as you could."

He wanted to scream at her to stop, but something told him to keep quiet and go along with her charade. At least the last part of what she'd told him was the truth. She *did* love him. He was certain of that.

"I understand," he said, and he reached out for her hand, but she pulled away.

"Now it's your turn, Harry."

"For what?"

"Who the hell is Diane Kinney?" She spoke the words carefully, letting each one convey her hurt and anger.

He'd been so obsessed with getting her to confess that he'd completely forgotten about the other woman.

"That's her, right there," he said, pointing to the magazine that lay on the desk.

Carol looked down at the pretty face on the cover. "And just how is she connected with all this?"

"I don't know."

"Then why is she on that list?"

"Because I think that I know her."

"What do you mean, you *think* that you know her? Either you do or you don't."

"Look, I know it sounds crazy, but when I saw that magazine in Simmons' office, I had an overwhelming feeling that I knew the woman."

"For Christ's sake, Harry, I never saw her before in my life. It just doesn't make any sense that you could know her."

"I can't help that. Maybe she has nothing to do with all this, but until I can find proof one way or the other, I've got to go with my feelings. Please try to understand that."

"What am I supposed to do? Wait around patiently until you find out whether or not you've been sleeping with some fashion model? The whole thing's ludicrous. I don't even believe it's happening."

"If you don't want me to stay here, I can check into a motel."

The suggestion caused a sudden shift in Carol's mood.

"I'm sorry," she said. "We're both under a strain. I guess we do need a change of scenery—but together."

Harry's instincts urged him to agree with her suggestion.

"That's a good idea. Where would you like to go?"

"Oh, I don't know. One of those New England villages on the coast might be nice; it's off-season, so the rates ought to be reasonable."

"That sounds fine."

"I'll go down to the travel agency right now and bring home some brochures. Okay?"

"Sure. Want me to come along?"

"No, I'd rather surprise you."

"Whatever you like."

Animation was beginning to return to her voice. "Well, I'd better go fix my face and be on my way." As she turned to leave, he called after her. "Carol?"

She looked back at him.

"Believe me, I wish none of this had happened."

"I know," she said. "But it'll all work out; I just know it will."

"I hope so."

She made no reply as she left the room.

On her way to the travel agency, Carol stopped at a public phone booth. The coins clanked into the money box, the tone came on the line, and she dialed.

"This is Carol. I need Sutherland."

She waited a few seconds and then spoke again. Her message was brief and to the point.

"He's discovered our girlfriend," she said. "I'm initiating Contingency Blue."

The reply at the other end of the line was affirmative.

Replacing the receiver, Carol stood alone inside the glass booth. She was smiling uncontrollably and put her hand over her mouth to stop it, because she knew that if she broke into a laugh she might easily start to cry. It was all so funny, in a terrible way, these games they were playing. Funny. Hysterically funny.

Carol felt a keen sense of betrayal at what she'd just done and realized that she was frightened for Harry. The plan was set in irretrievable motion, and no one, not even Sutherland, knew exactly how it would end. "You goddamn bastard, Sutherland," Carol whispered, then opened the door of the telephone booth and stepped back into the sunshine. Her face was perfectly calm, even cheerful. Any unsuspecting shopper would have been startled to hear her whisper, "You crummy bastard," as she crossed the street.

10

The woman looked like a Greek goddess. She stood framed by tall marble columns, the panels of her feathered gown dancing gently in the breeze. Her jet-black hair was woven into an intricate pattern of tight curls, its fullness accenting the high cheekbones and smoothly chiseled features of her face. From each ear a teardrop of gold and diamonds dangled above her bare shoulders.

Suddenly she began to move, striking one angular pose after another, while a man in his late thirties, his tan chest bared beneath his half-buttoned safari shirt, tracked her with the fast shutter of his camera.

"Beautiful, love," the photographer said. "Let's break for lunch."

Diane Kinney stepped down from the set. Hot lights clicked off; the wind machine ceased to ruffle the crimson plumage that draped her body. In a corner of the studio a telephone began to ring. The photographer crossed the room and answered it.

"Hello? Yes, she is; hold on a second."

Diane was bending over a small office refrigerator and removing a plastic container of orange juice.

"It's for you," the photographer said.

She set the bottle down on top of the fridge and picked up the phone.

"Hello?" Fear entered her when she heard the refined British accent at the other end of the line.

"I see," she said. "Yes, of course I can be there. Whatever you say. Fine. Good-bye."

She hung up the phone and decided not to hide her emotions.

"What's wrong?" the photographer asked.

"That was the hospital calling about my sister."

"I didn't know you had one."

"We were never very close. But now . . . they say she's dying. Some sort of blood disease."

"I'm sorry." The mention of death in the make-believe surroundings of his studio made him feel awkward.

"We'll have to finish up today. Can we do that?"

"Sure. I only need one more setup anyway."

"Thanks, Paul."

"Listen, if there's anything I can do . . ."

She managed to smile through her panic. "As a matter of fact, there is. I'd like to trade in my orange juice for some Scotch if you've got any."

"Coming right up." He walked over to a cabinet on the other side of the studio, but Diane was oblivious of his movements. She had too much on her mind. Things were in danger of falling apart. Less than forty-eight hours ago she'd gotten word that her part-time employers were very dissatisfied with her. She'd begged them for another chance, but their reply had been vague, much too vague. And what about Sutherland? Was he aware of her lucrative sideline, or was it all merely coincidence? Yet he had just personally called to give her her traveling orders; that had happened on only one other occasion during the three years of their relationship. At that time it had been a good omen, a sign of his trust in her. But what about now? She tried to steady herself, tell herself that she was jumping to conclusions.

The photographer returned with a tumbler of Scotch and some ice. She let the liquid burn its way down her throat and into her chest.

At least this Milford, whoever he was, sounded more interesting than the fat Arab in Dallas that Sutherland had assigned her last time. Diane took another gulp of Scotch. Its warmth told her there was no reason to be afraid, not yet, at least. Not until she arrived at Tarawaulk Bay.

* * *

After Carol left for the travel agency, Harry stretched out on the den sofa. His wife had lied to him twice in the past two days, and there was nothing he could do but follow her lead and hope to discover her reasons. Deception was something he'd never seen in her before, and even though he was certain she was doing it to protect him from the truth, her actions had weakened their relationship. He didn't like to admit it, but he felt he had to be on guard in her presence. He was actually a little bit afraid of the woman he'd loved for almost ten years.

His eyes began to close. He grew tired easily these days. Then, in the foggy world between sleep and wakefulness, a new image flashed across his mind. He lay there like a helpless victim waiting for the next blow, and it came again, this time lingering a split second longer, as if to reassure him that it was indeed real. Then it was over. Harry sat up and focused all his powers of concentration on recalling what he had seen. It wasn't difficult; the image was firmly rooted in his memory. An office door, that's what had come to him a few moments ago, a closed office door with a nameplate on it: J. McNEAL.

He turned the name over and over in his thoughts, straining to find the least bit of familiarity connected with it. But there was nothing. Moving to the desk, he wrote the name down and began rearranging the letters, on the assumption that it was an anagram. The combinations produced nothing but gibberish, causing him to throw down his pencil in disgust. Another piece of the puzzle had been dropped into his lap, and, as with the others, he didn't know how or where it would fit into the still-unfinished picture.

Harry reached for his list that still lay on top of the desk. Picking up a pencil, he added a fifth point to the column of Key Questions: Who is J. McNeal?

Carol arrived home from the travel agency buoyant with excitement.

"Come on in the living room, honey. I want to show you what I found."

Harry settled himself next to her on the sofa and watched as she withdrew a brochure from her purse.

"I fell in love with the place the minute the agent showed it to me," she said. "Isn't it beautiful?"

Together they turned the multicolored pages that depicted one picturesque New England scene after another. There was boating and fishing, foot trails that wound through lush green woods, a glorious beach outlined with glistening white sand, comfortable cottages—each with its own fireplace, and some with up to three bedrooms—and a rustic lodge that boasted some of the finest cuisine on the coast.

"It looks marvelous," Harry said.

"Doesn't it, though? Actually, it's rather an exclusive place, but it does stay open in the off-season, and of course the rates are much cheaper now. We could have a wonderful time there; I just know we could."

He smiled at her enthusiasm, reminded of how relaxed they used to be together.

"Are you sure this is the place you want?" he asked.

"I'm sure. But you have to like it, too."

"I do."

"Really? I don't want to drag you someplace where you'll be unhappy."

"Listen, we're doing this for relaxation. If you're happy, I'm happy."

She threw her arms around him and kissed him on the cheek. "I haven't been so excited since . . . I don't know when."

"You must be. This looks like the only brochure you brought home."

She looked at him sheepishly. "I'm afraid that's not all I did."

"Oh?"

"I already made a reservation for us—a one-bedroom cottage with its own private boat dock. And it's within walking distance of the lodge."

"You think of everything. When do we leave?"

"Tomorrow morning. You're not angry?"

"Of course not. We agreed to go away, didn't we?"

"I know, but I really didn't give you any choice."

"The place sounds terrific. I'm sure it'll do us both a lot of good."

"I'm glad you feel that way, because I want this to be a new beginning."

"Maybe it will be. Maybe I'll learn what's been causing all these . . . things that have been happening to me, and the two of us can pick up where we left off a few days ago."

Carol looked at him, and for an instant her eyes held a terrible sadness. "I hope so."

"Hey," he said, breaking the uncomfortable silence, "how about some lunch?"

"You bet. How hungry are you?"

"Starved."

"Good. There's some roast beef left from last night. And I bought some French rolls at the bakery this morning."

"Great. We got any Swiss cheese?"

"I think so."

"Then put 'em all together with some chili sauce and a tall glass of iced tea."

"I'm on my way," she said, and walked into the kitchen.

When she'd left the room, Harry picked up the brochure and began thumbing through it. Though he was glad to see her excited about their going away, he had a strong feeling that her selection of the resort must somehow be tied in with whatever it was she was holding back from him. In any event, he'd find out soon enough when they got to this place called—what was it again? He flipped to the front of the brochure. Oh, yes, Tarawaulk Bay.

11

For once, a brochure hadn't lied. Tarawaulk Bay was every bit as lovely as its publicity had promised. The lodge rested on the crest of a grassy knoll that sloped up gently from the perimeter of the beach. Harry pulled into the adjacent parking lot, and they surveyed the scene below them. A few sailboats dotted the calm water of the bay. The beach itself was deserted, save for the generously spaced waterfront cottages that sat on their sturdy pilings. The broad expanse of clean white sand gradually gave way to an autumn-colored woods that rimmed the southern portion of the inlet.

Carol let out a slow, relaxed breath. "It's just as I hoped it would be. Don't you think so?"

"Exactly. Couldn't be better."

"Harry?"

"Yeah?"

"Are you glad we came?"

"Of course I am. Honey, is there something on your mind?"

"Just that I love you."

"I love you, too." He reached over and patted her knee. "Everything's going to be fine."

"I know."

"Let's go and check in, okay?"

"I'm right behind you," she said. The forced gaiety in her voice was obvious.

Cottage number four was a leisurely five-minute walk from the lodge. It had its own private dock with a small rowboat tied up to it, and high tide carried white foam to within a few feet of the wooden steps that led up to the porch.

Inside, the front room was dominated by a massive brick fireplace. The single bedroom held its queen-size bed with ease, and the bath offered both a tub and a stall shower.

The bellman hoisted the suitcases onto the two aluminum racks at the foot of the bed, and Harry pressed two dollars into the young man's hand.

"Yes, sir," the bellman said. "If you need anything, just dial six on the phone. That connects you right with the desk."

"Thanks," Harry said.

"Enjoy your stay," the young man said as he left.

"We will."

Carol opened a window, and the scent of the sea air filled the bedroom. When she turned around, there was an unmistakable invitation on her face.

"This is too good to waste," she said. "Let's enjoy it while we can." She began to unbutton her dress.

Harry indicated the open window. "Are we going to perform for the natives?"

Carol slid her dress over her hips and let it fall to the floor. "To hell with them," she said simply, and lay down on the bed.

They awoke in the soft light of sunset. Harry snuggled the covers up around his wife's shoulders. Her eyes were still heavy with sleep.

"How are you?" he asked.

"Wonderful."

"We slept away the afternoon."

"Good. We needed it. You feel all right?"

"Fine."

They lay there in silence for a little while; then she said, "You know what I think?"

"What?"

"This place is going to make everything good again."

Until she said that, he'd almost forgotten why they were there. She shifted her position, and the covers slid down slightly, exposing the fullness of a breast. A tenseness came over Harry, as though he'd been caught in bed with a strange woman.

"I think I'll get cleaned up for dinner," he said.

"Take your time; I may never want to leave this bed."

All the while he was shaving, he couldn't shake the absurd feeling of guilt that nagged at the back of his mind. Why should making love to his wife leave him feeling this way?—especially since he'd slept a sound, peaceful sleep, untroubled by the nightmare. He decided it was just a symptom of nerves. After all, their time here would be a critical point in his search; if she refused to volunteer whatever information she had, it would trigger an ugly confrontation, leaving a memory of distrust they'd have to share for the rest of their lives.

Standing under the steaming shower, he got his emotions under control. A few minutes later he entered the bedroom, to find Carol dozing restlessly. When he put on his slacks and shirt and she still hadn't awakened, he bent over and kissed her softly. Her eyes opened with a start, and for a moment she looked at him with a grave sense of alarm.

"Take it easy," he said. "It's just me."

"Sorry; you startled me."

"You were tossing and turning. Everything okay?"

"I must have been dreaming." She sat up and wiped her forehead with the back of her hand. Her face was damp.

"Please, one of us is enough on that score."

"That's for sure." She laughed.

"So tell me, do you plan to get up for dinner, or do we live on love for the next few days?"

"What *I'd* love is a nice hot bath. Why don't you go on ahead to the lodge and have a drink? I'll meet you in the dining room in half an hour. Do you mind?"

"Sounds all right, except for one thing."

"What?"

"You're still in bed."

"I'll get up," she said teasingly.

"Uh-huh. Famous last words."

"I will; I promise."

Carol started to giggle, and Harry lunged at the sheets. She grabbed his wrists, and the two of them grew weak with laughter. He finally pulled loose and threw the covers back.

"Out," he said, gesturing with his thumb toward the bathroom.

She stood naked in front of him.

"That's a lovely outfit you have on."

"If you don't get out of here, I'm going to wear it to dinner."

"You know, that might almost be worth it."

"Good-bye, Harry."

He walked to the bedroom door and then turned around. "The trouble with you is, you don't have any spirit of adventure."

"I'll see you in half an hour, dear," she called from the bathroom, "with or without my clothes."

Stepping out onto the front porch, Harry stood and watched the waves wash up on the beach. He felt good. He couldn't remember the last time he and Carol had joked like that. Hopefully, it would soon be a constant part of their lives again.

The cocktail lounge was dimly lit and sparsely populated. Rough-hewn beams crisscrossed the lofty ceiling. A flickering hurricane lamp sat atop each tiny table. There was only one waitress on duty, and she stood chatting with the bartender, a gray-haired man who masked his boredom behind a congenial-looking face. The bar was a long, lazy-S affair; Harry walked up to one of the many vacant stools and sat down. The bartender hesitated just long enough to show his New England independence, then came to take the order.

"Good evening. What'll it be?"

"Vodka martini, straight up." It had been a long time since he'd had one of those, but he felt in the mood for a change. There was a dish of peanuts nearby, and he reached out and grabbed a handful.

His drink arrived, icy cold and with two olives. He took a

sip and set it back on the little square of napkin in front of him. Since he hadn't eaten in hours, the mixture raced through his system with maximum impact. He could feel the fog beginning to swirl through his head, but it didn't matter. The scene in their cottage a few minutes ago had him convinced that Carol was on the verge of a confession, and once that happened, he'd really feel as if he were in control of the situation. Then they'd be working together, and it would be just a matter of time until his riddle was solved.

Harry took some more peanuts and washed them down with another sip of his drink. Tarawaulk Bay was going to be the turning point of his investigation. He was certain of it.

"Is this seat taken?" Considering the emptiness of the place, it was a line right out of an old Bogart picture, and Harry was just about to toss out an appropriate reply to the young woman when he suddenly realized whom he was looking at. His voice stuck in his throat.

"I said, 'Do you mind if I sit here?' " Diane Kinney looked into Harry's face with calm, unwavering eyes.

"No; help yourself," he said, quite aware that he must have looked like a gaping adolescent as he watched her slide onto the stool and cross her legs. She wore a soft-beige knit dress trimmed at the cuffs and hemline in chocolate brown. A strand of large mocha beads interspaced with bold golden links encircled her neck.

"Yes, ma'am. What's your pleasure?" the bartender asked.

"Scotch on the rocks."

In an instant her drink was ready.

"Put it on my check," Harry said. The words came too fast and sounded awkward. His mind was racing in confusion and disbelief. That Diane Kinney would be here, the one person he was looking for, in the resort that Carol had chosen, seemed too miraculous a coincidence to accept without question. Harry suspected that if he challenged her directly, she would just laugh and shrug her shoulders, and he would be that much farther from learning the truth. He would have to venture slowly.

"There's no need to do that," Diane said. "I can pay for it."

"Please. I'm . . . I'm kind of celebrating tonight."

"Okay; thanks."

"Cheers," he said.

"Cheers." They raised their glasses and drank.

"Is it your birthday or something?" she asked.

"What?" He was trying to find a casual way to say she looked familiar, and he hadn't heard the question.

"You said you were celebrating. I thought maybe it was your birthday."

"Oh, no. Nothing like that."

"Well, whatever the reason, I appreciate the drink."

"You're very welcome." Harry took a deep breath. "Excuse me, but—this sounds terrible—but you look very familiar. What I mean is, I remember seeing your picture on a magazine cover. Are you Diane Kinney?"

"Yes, I am; but how do you know my name?"

"I looked up the credit on the inside."

"That's very flattering. Not many people bother to do that, Mr. . . ."

"I'm Harry Milford."

"I'm very glad to know you, Mr. Milford. You make a girl feel good." She didn't show the slightest hint of recognition when he mentioned his name.

"What brings you to Tarawaulk Bay?" he asked nonchalantly.

"Just a few days' rest between assignments."

"This is my first time here. We just got in today."

"We?"

"My wife, Carol, and I." Again, not even a flicker of recognition showed on her face.

"You'll love it; it's an absolutely marvelous place. In fact, I actually prefer this time of the year to the season. Crowds bore me."

"I know what you mean; I don't like them much myself. I can't relax when everybody around me is working hard at having a good time."

"You're a kindred soul." She took a healthy swallow of Scotch.

"Miss Kinney . . . or is it Ms.?"

"Diane."

"Listen, Diane, please don't think this is some kind of a line, but haven't we met before?"

"I don't think so, but anything's possible."

"It's just that I really feel that we have," he persisted, hoping for some kind of acknowledgment.

"Then maybe we did." She took the swizzle stick from her drink, wrapped it in the paper cocktail napkin, and put it in her purse. "It's a crazy habit of mine, but I've got a hell of a collection."

Harry could see that she was getting ready to leave. He decided to play his last card. "My wife will be here in a few minutes; would you care to join us for dinner? She'd be very interested to meet a fashion model."

"Thanks, but I've already eaten. When I get away like this, the luxury of an early meal and a good night's sleep is more than I can turn down. But I'm sure we'll be running into each other. I'm in cottage nine."

"We're in number four."

"Thanks again for the drink," she said, and pressed her hand on his thigh as she got up to leave.

She disappeared through the entrance, and Harry had all he could do to keep from running after her and demanding that she tell him where they had met, what she knew about Carol, why she was really at Tarawaulk Bay. As he turned back to his drink, something caught the corner of his eye. He looked down at his lap. A small piece of white paper lay on his thigh where she had touched him. Apparently she'd removed it from her purse when she took the swizzle stick. He picked up the paper and was proud of his low-key reaction as he read the message: "My cottage. 12:30 tonight."

He crumpled it and put it in his pocket. Then he finished the rest of his martini in one long, triumphant swallow. Only when he put it down did he see that his hand was trembling.

* * *

A short distance away, on the other side of the wall that separated the cocktail lounge from the main lobby, an athletic-looking man in his early thirties approached the desk. A bellman walked behind him carrying two large suitcases. The gentleman himself gripped a slim, black attaché case in his left hand.

"I hope I'm not disturbing you."

The night manager looked up from what was apparently a very slow game of solitaire. "No, not at all, sir. Can I help you?"

"My name is Powers. I have a reservation for cottage number eight." The man spoke with a slight trace of an accent.

The manager put down his cards and quickly checked the list. "Yes, Mr. Powers. Just fill this out, please." He swiveled the registration card toward him. Powers completed the form quickly.

"Cottage number eight for Mr. Powers," the night manager said as he handed the key across to the bellman. "I'm sure you'll find everything you'll need, sir. Extra sheets and pillowcases on the middle shelf in the hall closet."

With a curt nod of the head, Powers was gone. The manager returned to his cards, smiling slightly as he laid the black jack on the red queen.

When he was sure the bellman was many yards away, Powers started to unpack. From one suitcase he withdrew a black wet suit, face mask, leaded weight belt, depth gauge, and a pair of flippers. From the other suitcase he lifted a black scuba tank and mouthpiece. The air tank contained thirty minutes of oxygen.

Then he opened the attaché case. It was lined with green felt and held, in three form-fitting impressions, a custom-made .45-caliber automatic, a silencer, and a telescopic Star-Scope designed for sighting a target in darkness.

Impassively, Powers began a thorough and efficient inspection of his equipment.

12

Harry paid for the two drinks, left a tip on the bar, and walked through the cocktail lounge into the dining room. Though only scattered tables were occupied, the maître d' approached him with cool indifference.

"Good evening, sir. A table for one?"

"Two. My wife will be joining me shortly."

"Very good. Right this way, please."

The maître d' threaded his way between tables and led Harry to a corner booth by the window that overlooked the dim beach below.

"You'll bring Mrs. Milford over when she arrives?"

"Certainly. May I order you a cocktail while you wait?"

"Vodka martini, straight up."

"Thank you. Enjoy your evening."

Left alone, Harry slipped his hand into his coat pocket and felt the crumpled message Diane Kinney had given him. The touch of the paper against his skin brought all the excitement he'd managed to hold back when he first read it. He looked at his watch; six and one-half hours stood between him and a key piece of the puzzle. He knew it would probably be the longest interval of his life.

Soon his drink arrived, and as he took his first sip, the questions began to seep into his mind. What was Diane Kinney's *real* line of work? Was he connected with it in any way? Did she know who J. McNeal was? How deeply was Carol involved in all this? Was something planned to happen at Tarawaulk Bay? Through the window he could make out the silhouettes of some of the cottages. He tried to figure out which one was number nine, but it was impossible.

A movement across the room attracted his attention, and he turned, to see the maître d' leading Carol to his table. She looked lovely in a camel-colored skirt and navy-blue turtleneck top, a butterfly pin of red enamel and diamonds above her left breast. Harry stood to greet her as the maître d' deftly pulled out the tabletop to ease her entrance. No, Harry thought again. She loves me. I must be going crazy to suspect her. When they were seated, she ordered a whiskey sour, the menus were placed on a corner of the table, and Harry was face-to-face with his wife. She looked so happy that he decided to leave the questions until after dinner.

"You look terrific," he said.

"Not only that, I'm on time."

"I'm impressed."

"You should be; I had to use every ounce of willpower to get out of that tub."

"Thanks a lot. Have I always come in second to a bathtub?"

"Unfair. No matter how I answer that, I lose."

"You mean *I* do. A guy likes to think he ranks somewhere ahead of the bathroom fixtures."

"How many drinks did you have while you were waiting for me, anyway?"

"This is only number two, but I happen to be feeling very good."

"Me too," she said. "This is going to be a good night for us."

Harry thought he detected a touch of wistfulness in her words, but before he could say anything, their waiter brought her drink.

"Would you like to order now?" he asked Harry.

"I know what I want without even looking," Carol said. She turned to the waiter. "Do you have steamed whole lobster?"

"Certainly."

"That's what I'll have—with some clam chowder to begin," she added.

"Make it two," Harry said.

The waiter scribbled the order on a small pad. "Would you care for any wine?"

Harry looked across the table at Carol.

"Why not?" she said.

"I'll leave the selection up to you," he told the waiter.

"Fine. Thank you very much, sir."

"I hope this doesn't come to more than five dollars and thirty-seven cents," Harry joked when the waiter had gone.

"You're a nut." Carol raised her glass in a toast. "To our new beginning."

"I'll drink to that."

Dinner progressed in a stream of pleasant, lighthearted conversation. Though Carol drank more than she usually did, Harry noticed that it didn't seem to bother her. He decided she was using it to give her the courage to tell him what she knew. Once or twice during the meal he'd considered making it easy on her and telling her about his meeting with Diane Kinney. But he wanted the honesty to return to their marriage, and it had to come from her.

Some ninety minutes after the first course had been set in front of them, they finished their coffee and leaned back against the cushioned vinyl of the booth.

"That was fantastic," Carol said. "I may never walk again."

"You did pretty well for yourself."

"Will you still love me two pounds heavier?"

"Right here?"

"Don't tempt me; after all that wine, I'm liable to do anything."

"Somehow, I don't think the New England folk would appreciate it."

"Then the New England folk have a lot to learn about fun."

Harry scanned the check and laid thirty dollars on the table. "Shall we go?"

"I'll try, but I'm not guaranteeing anything."

The maître d' bade them good evening as they left. They

passed through the lobby and stepped out on the spacious deck that rimmed the lodge. The sky was clear and dotted with stars. A gibbous moon hung low on the horizon. The night air was cool and tinged with dampness, but comfortable.

"How about a walk along the beach?" Harry asked.

"I'd love it."

They leisurely descended the well-lit stairs that ran down the knoll. When they reached the sand, Carol stooped to remove her shoes.

"Won't that ruin your stockings?"

"Probably. But it feels good."

She took his arm, and they started out across the beach, in the opposite direction from their cottage. As they walked, Harry noticed that the numbers on the cottages were going up. Carol rambled on about how relaxed she felt and how beautiful the night was. He let the conversation run in whatever direction she wanted, determined to let her pick the moment when she'd make her confession. After a few minutes she stopped and stood looking out at the bay. Harry had been keeping track of the cottages as they passed; they were standing directly in front of number nine.

The gentle lapping of the surf marked the silence between them. He moved behind her and put his arms around her; she leaned back against him.

"What are you thinking about?" he whispered.

"How peaceful and uncomplicated it is—right here, right now. I wish it could stay like this forever."

"Maybe it can."

"No," she said matter-of-factly. "We just have to enjoy it when it comes along."

He turned her around and kissed her.

"I love you, Carol."

"Let's walk back to our place." There was a subtle shift in her mood, as if she'd gone on the defensive. Harry put his arm around her, and they began the walk back. He looked down at the sand as they moved along the beach, realizing that the moment had come and gone, and that she was going to tell him nothing. By the time they'd reached their cottage, he'd made up his mind to take the initiative.

She started to turn toward the steps leading up to the porch, but he put his hand on her shoulder and stopped her. The wooden dock with its moored rowboat lay a few yards behind them.

"Let's go out in the boat," he said.

Her eyes widened in astonishment. "You're kidding. Now?"

"Sure. Why not?"

"But it's pitch black out there."

"I won't go far; it'll be nice."

She hesitated. "Okay, if you really want to."

"I do."

He held her hand as she bent over and slipped on her shoes. The vacant night absorbed the sound of their footsteps on the sea-worn planks. Harry hooked a gaff into a small cleat on the side of the boat and pulled it even with the dock. Holding it steady, he extended his other hand to Carol and eased her down into the tiny craft; then he stepped in beside her. He cast off the single line and settled himself across from her on the oarsman's seat. It had been quite a while since he'd been out in a boat, but the rhythm of the stroke soon came back to him, and before long they were twenty-five or thirty yards offshore. Then he stopped rowing and let the boat drift on the gentle swells of the bay. They were in an envelope of darkness. The lights of the lodge and cottages twinkled over Carol's shoulders. He could barely see her face. All the way out, neither of them had said a word.

"Carol, this isn't easy for me, but you leave me no choice. Tell me what you know."

"About what?"

"Please; no more games. I want to find out what's been happening to me, but I also want to preserve our marriage. So be honest with me."

"I am being honest with you. Why do you think I know something?"

"Because you lied to me, for one thing, and there's something strange about this resort, for another."

"I don't know what you're talking about, Harry. And I'm getting cold. Let's go back in."

"You weren't talking to Sue Martin on the telephone that day, and you weren't talking to Dr. Simmons, either."

"Of course I was. I told you; I called him to find out if you'd kept anything from me. Why don't you believe me?"

"Because the number you called was in Washington, D.C."

"That's ridiculous."

"For God's sake, Carol, I verified it through the phone company! Why are you carrying on like this? Just tell me the truth; is that too much to ask?"

"I am telling you the truth! I don't know who the hell you talked to at the phone company, but they gave you wrong information. So who are you going to believe, your wife or some screwed-up computer?"

Harry felt totally lost. She sounded so convincing, and the Washington number *had* been out of service. Why hadn't he called Simmons' office to check out her story? That had been stupid of him, but there was nothing he could do about it now. If she were telling the truth, what would she think of him for accusing her this way?

"Well?" she asked. "Do you still think I'm holding out on you?"

"I don't want to."

"That's not an answer."

"I can always call Simmons' office tomorrow and find out."

"I'll dial the goddamn number for you. But I want to know *now* if you trust me."

"There's something else."

"What?"

"Diane Kinney. She's here, at Tarawaulk Bay—cottage number nine."

There was a long pause before Carol spoke. "I don't believe you."

"I was face-to-face with her before dinner this evening."

"You mean somebody you *thought* was her."

"What are you trying to do? Convince me that I'm losing my mind?"

"I'm suggesting that you were the victim of a coincidence."

"No good. She told me her name. And she wants to see me."

"Where?"

"In her cottage. I'm to be there at twelve-thirty tonight. Alone." He hesitated, then continued, "You picked this resort. Be honest with me, Carol. What's going on? What aren't you telling me?"

"Harry, listen to me, don't you see what's happening?" Carol leaned forward and laid her hand on his knee. "This is a nice place, a well-known place. We're here, and this woman who looks familiar, probably because you saw her once on a TV commercial or something, is here, too. Does that add up to a plot? Think about it. You're scared, we're both scared, but we have to stick together. You can't let your mind get poisoned by all this suspicion."

Harry listened. He could almost believe her. "I have to go to her cabin, though," he said. "Just to see."

"And what do you expect me to say to that?"

"You could tell me why she's here."

"I don't know, I tell you!" Then, furious: "Damnit, I just don't know! What do you want from me? To let you meet some strange woman in her cottage in the middle of the night? Just what the hell do you hope to prove by that?"

"That she has the answers I'm looking for." Harry felt strangely calm now.

"And what if she doesn't know anything?"

"If it turns out that I've never met her, if she's just looking for a night's recreation, then we might as well check out of here tomorrow morning and let Simmons put me in the hospital."

For almost a full minute they rode the rise and fall of the boat in silence.

"I wish you luck, Harry," Carol finally said. "I really do."

There was no sound except the low slapping of the waves, then a creak as Harry grasped the oars and began to row back to shore.

The luminous dial on his watch read twelve twenty-eight and thirty-two seconds as he climbed the steps up to the porch of cottage number nine. Never in his life had Harry been so acutely aware of time, or of himself. This first half-hour of the morning was still and cold. He wiped his sweaty palms on his trousers, then raised his right hand and knocked on the door. The sound seemed to leap back at him, announcing his presence to the entire beach. A light suddenly filtered out through the closed draperies of a front window. The muffled sounds of footsteps could be heard from within. Tentatively, the door opened to the narrow width of the restraining chain that was bolted from the inside. A vertical slash of lips, nose, and eyes peered out at him. Then the door quickly closed, the chain was unfastened, and Diane Kinney stood in front of him.

"Come in, Mr. Milford," she said.

He stepped inside, and she closed the door behind him. He stood there like a virgin in the lobby of a brothel, waiting to be undone. She wore a pale-blue satin robe that hung to the floor. Matching slippers could be glimpsed beneath the hemline. She was a strikingly beautiful woman, but that didn't allow Harry to forget why he was there.

"You're prompt," she said.

"I try to be."

"We'd better make this as quick as possible. Give me the merchandise and my instructions."

He looked at her as if she were speaking a foreign language, then caught himself.

"First I have some questions," he said.

"Questions? What questions?"

"What type of merchandise am I supposed to deliver to you?"

"How should I know that? I'm never told those things in advance."

"Where have we met before?"

"We've never met before."

"You're lying."

"Did Sutherland put you up to this? Well, you can tell him I'm clean. So, if you have nothing for me, I'll say good night, Mr. Milford."

"Who's J. McNeal?" Harry persisted, his voice harsh and cutting.

"I don't know!"

"Answer my questions, damnit!" He reached out and grabbed her hard by the shoulders.

"All right," she said. "You're hurting me."

He released her, leaving the satin wrinkled from the pressure of his grip. He'd never been rough with a woman, and he wasn't pleased with himself. But at last he was going to get his answers.

Diane walked over to the sofa and sat down. As she crossed her legs, the unbuttoned portion of the robe fell away, exposing bare skin from her upper thigh to her ankle. Harry's eyes inadvertently followed the curve of her leg, just as she knew any man's would do. In the short space of that distraction, she withdrew the snubnosed .38 from behind a throw cushion on the sofa and aimed it at Harry's chest.

"I don't know who you are, Milford, but you just got yourself into one hell of a lot of trouble."

"Look, I didn't mean to hurt you; I never had any intention of doing anything like that. I just need the answers to those questions. You have no idea how important they are to me. Please, you've got to help me."

"I'm not interested." She picked up the telephone that rested in front of her on the coffee table.

"What are you going to do?"

"I'm going to call the night manager and report an attempted rape. Sound good?"

"It won't work."

"Oh? And why not?"

"Because my wife knows that I'm here. Would it make sense that I'd tell her I was coming if I'd planned to rape you?"

"Stranger things have happened." She squeezed the telephone receiver between her left shoulder and ear and moved her finger to dial.

"Sutherland won't like it." Harry said. He hadn't the slightest idea who Sutherland was, but she'd mentioned his name with the implication that he was someone important.

It worked. She returned the receiver to the cradle.

"So this *was* one of his gambits," she said.

"Like you said—to see if you were clean."

"And you don't have anything for me?"

"Nothing."

Still holding the gun on him, she stood and walked to the front door. She opened it a crack and checked outside.

"Okay," she said. "Get the hell out of here." She stepped back and opened the door wide.

For a split second she stood framed in the threshold against the black night. Then, from a few yards beyond the porch came a faint, dull pop—a sound not unlike the flat of a hand slapping against a thick pillow. The next instant, the right side of Diane's head exploded outward in a thick shower of hair, bone, and brains. Her body thudded to the floor, shielding the gaping wound. Harry stood transfixed at the sight. Her eyes were still open; her face was frozen with indelible surprise.

By now Powers was already knee-deep in the surf, the gun wedged tightly between his weight belt and his firm stomach. He was pleased with the way it had gone, though he had been fully prepared to enter the woman's cottage to carry out his assignment.

He took a last quick sighting on the dim light of the cabin cruiser that was moored just beyond the inlet of the bay; then he lowered his face mask and disappeared into the water.

13

Harry raced from the cottage, through the wide-open front door that stood as silent testimony to the last willful act of Diane Kinney. He tripped running down the steps, his chest slamming hard into the beach and the breath rushing out of his lungs. The impact acted as a brake on the blurring speed of his thoughts. Raising himself on his elbows, he spat sand from his mouth. Only half of him believed what he had seen less than a minute ago. He had been witness to murder. A life had ended in front of his eyes. It was then that it occurred to Harry that perhaps he was to be next; and the idea that any one of the coming seconds might find him dead forced him to his feet.

For a frenzied moment he forgot in which direction his cottage lay; then he spotted its lone light far down the beach and began to run. In the beginning, he expected every stride to be his last. His muscles were taut, braced for the impact of a bullet that would send him tumbling to the ground. He tried to anticipate the pain it would bring if the assassin's aim were faulty, and found himself forming a perverse prayer to steady the nameless man's hand.

He pushed on, arms and legs pumping, his breath coming in increasingly shorter gasps. But somewhere along the line he realized he wasn't trying to outrace death. If whoever had killed Diane had also wanted Harry dead, it would have been accomplished the moment he'd stepped out on the porch of cottage number nine. Then the macabre thought that he *had* been shot skimmed across his mind. Was his body still lying back there at the foot of the steps? Was this sensation of escape merely a reflex fantasy filling up the final seconds of his life? No; the gathering pain in his lungs told him his flight was real. He had to get to Carol and tell her what had happened. The light in their cottage grew gradually brighter and closer.

Suddenly his dim view of the landscape was blotted out, and an image from the nightmare flashed in front of his eyes. It was gone in an instant, but reappeared again and again, causing him to lose his momentum and struggle to regain his balance. Though he'd become relatively used to the images, this one had a particularly eerie effect. It was as if Harry were seeing himself in another dimension, because the scene that was flashing before him was of himself running in the nightmare, just as he was now. And with it came one of his answers: the unidentifiable substance that had impeded his progress in the dream was exactly what he was fighting against at this moment—sand.

But why? Had the nightmare and the other images been an extended form of precognition foretelling the murder of Diane Kinney? Is that why people were chasing him in the dream? Had they thought him the guilty one? Harry was compelled to glance over his shoulder to see if he were being followed, but only the vacant shoreline stretched out behind him.

He continued to run, legs aching from the strain, the fatigue of his body keeping him from putting this new clue into proper perspective. His mouth was unbearably dry; his chest heaved from the labor of breathing. Then the pain began, entering from the back of his neck and spreading up his skull like the random pattern of colored veins in a slab of marble. It quickly grew in intensity, causing his vision to blur and bringing the onset of dizziness. He felt himself begin to weave uncontrollably, and then a cold splash of water against his ankles told him he'd strayed into the surf. He came to a halt and stood reeling at the water's edge. The light from his cottage was near now, and he began to stumble toward it, the palms of his hands pressed against the sides of his head in an effort to squeeze out the pain.

As he moved across the sand, the other pieces of his puzzle

danced before him in teasing frustration. The elevator panel with its glowing number twenty-two appeared and then began to rotate on an axis until it was nothing more than a pencil-thin line tracing a red circle in the air. The elaborate fountain spewed its multicolored jets of water high above him. The computer tapes spun uncontrollably; the bells clanged deafeningly in their lofty tower. And overlaying it all was a large-scale transparency of Diane Kinney's face, her wide eyes staring unbelievingly at the recognition of death.

Harry forced his way through this barrage of apparitions, staggering across the beach toward his cottage. Then he thought he saw the front door open and a figure step out on the porch, but he could no longer trust his senses. It took all his strength to put one foot in front of the other. Whether that was Carol standing up there, or someone waiting to accuse him of murder, or another one of his phantoms no longer made any difference to him. His body was a capsule of pain; his mind was a generator gone wild.

Unable to take another step, he sank to his knees, his hands still clasped tightly to the sides of his head.

Carol swiftly descended the wooden steps from the porch and hurried across the sand to him. She knelt down, her arms drawing him next to her. The touch of her skin was cool, and he looked up into her face. The nightmare images had fled, and he saw that her eyes were filling with tears. Tentatively, Harry raised a hand and lightly brushed her cheek; he felt the gentle pressure of her lips against his forehead in reply. Desperate to share his terrible knowledge, he opened his mouth to speak, to tell her what had happened in cottage number nine, but all that emerged was a deep, guttural sound. Then he passed out in his wife's arms.

14

Harry drifted in the limbo of half-sleep. Thoughts slipped in and out of focus, none of them lingering long enough to be called rational. Then, slowly, reality began to take over, and he realized that he was lying in bed, flat on his back, with the covers pulled up to his neck. Somehow Carol must have gotten him up the steps and into their cottage. He opened his eyes and was greeted by heavy, impenetrable darkness. His head felt as if it were packed with cotton. He wondered how long he'd been asleep—whether this was still the blackness of early morning or the night of a lost day. Routinely, he started to raise his left arm for a glance at his watch, but nothing happened. He tried it again, and again there was no response. Though the muscles tensed in his arm, the limb remained motionless against the mattress. A palpable lump of fear settled in his chest as he got the same results—or lack of them—with his other arm and both legs. He tried to raise his head and found that he could, though it was a strain on his neck, and he soon had to lie back down on the pillow. Harry looked unblinkingly into the darkness as the terror mounted inside him. Then he became aware of something that carried the promise of hope: his right hand was clenched tightly in a fist. Cautiously, he willed the fingers to open, and they obeyed. He quickly repeated the motion several times with each hand, and though his sense perception was still fuzzy, he found that he could also wiggle his toes and that he had limited lateral movement in both feet.

"Carol." He had to force himself not to shout her name like

a cry for help. "Carol," he called again, louder this time, but still with some semblance of calm. It would do no good to bring her racing into the room; two frightened people would be of little use to each other.

He was just about to call for the third time when he heard footsteps approaching. But the sound brought no relief, because as he lay wrapped in the darkness he could tell that *two* people were coming to answer his call.

The next instant, the door opened and the room was flooded with bright light that caused Harry to wince and turn his head away. When he opened his eyes again, a doctor and nurse were standing next to his bed, and he looked up at them in bewilderment.

"Hello, Mr. Milford. I'm Dr. Ordway, and this is Miss Styles. How are you feeling?"

"Where am I?"

"At a private clinic."

"Near Tarawaulk Bay?"

"Not far," Ordway said. "But it's important that you answer our questions. Are you in any pain?"

"I'm partially paralyzed." Harry was surprised at how flat his voice sounded. "I can't seem to move my arms or legs."

Ordway glanced briefly at the nurse; then he reached out and pulled down the bed covers.

"There's the cause of your paralysis, Mr. Milford."

Harry followed the doctor's pointing finger and saw that a padded leather restraint held his arm firmly to the mattress.

"They're on your legs, too," Ordway said. "You became violently delirious during the night. Believe me, it was done for your own good."

Harry's face reddened in embarrassment. Delirious. Strapped to his bed like a lunatic.

"How long have I been here?"

Ordway looked at his watch. "Just about ten hours."

"And was I delirious all that time?"

"For a good portion of it."

Harry had to learn if he'd blurted out anything about the murder. "What kind of things was I saying?" He tried to make the question sound as casual as possible.

"We'll talk about that later," the doctor said.

Was there a hint of patronage in his reply? Harry couldn't tell for sure.

"Can you undo these?" Harry indicated the restraints. "I promise I won't cause any trouble."

"I think we can arrange that." He and Miss Styles quickly removed the straps that fastened the restraints.

"There," the nurse said as she freed his left leg, "I'll bet that feels better."

Harry flexed his arms and legs, thankful for the simple act of muscle control. "That was a hell of a scare, to wake up and not be able to move."

"That's why we left your intercom switch open," Ordway said. "We wanted to be immediately available to reassure you."

"Thanks. A few minutes alone in the dark like that, and you could have fed me pablum for the rest of my life."

The doctor smiled as he hooked his stethoscope into his ears. "Let's have a listen and see how you're doing."

The cold touch of the metal disk against Harry's chest made him twitch. Out of the corner of his eye he noticed Miss Styles walk across to the window; then he heard the sound of the heavy blackout draperies opening, and the late-morning sunlight mingled with the harsh illumination of his room.

Dr. Ordway removed the stethoscope from his ears and let it dangle from his neck.

"Well?" Harry asked. Miss Styles now stood on the opposite side of his bed and began to take his pulse.

"Your chest is clear," the doctor said.

"And what about my heart?"

"It seems to be fine."

"Then there's no reason for me to stay here. Right?"

"There are still some tests I want to run. You were in the

midst of a major trauma when you were brought in this morning. I'd like to find out why. Is there anything you can tell me?''

Harry wanted to explain, very calmly, that he'd been talking to a beautiful young woman and somebody had blown the side of her head off. That's where his trauma had come from.

The nurse was taking his blood pressure, and Dr. Ordway was looking at him and waiting for an answer.

''I blacked out,'' Harry said. ''That's about all I remember.''

''Were there any noticeable symptoms beforehand?''

''No,'' he lied.

''Do you know why you were out on the beach at that time of night?''

''I couldn't sleep, so I'd gone for a walk.'' Apparently Carol had kept her explanations to a minimum, and he was glad. Then it occurred to him that perhaps Ordway knew everything and was testing him. There was only one way to find out; Carol would be honest with him. At least, he hoped so.

''I'd like to see my wife,'' he said.

Miss Styles had finished taking his blood pressure and was unwrapping the rubber strip from around Harry's arm. At the mention of his wife, she stopped what she was doing and looked across at the doctor.

''We weren't aware that you were married,'' Ordway said.

''Of course I'm married. My wife's name is Carol. You must have spoken to her when I was brought in.''

''No; we weren't on duty at that time.''

''Oh. Well, whoever was must have sent her back to the cottage to get some rest; it's number four over at Tarawaulk Bay.''

''I doubt that, Mr. Milford.''

''What do you mean? Where else could she be?''

''What the doctor is trying to tell you,'' Miss Styles said, ''is that your driver's license and other personal effects list you as a single man.''

''Then you must have looked at the wrong driver's license,

damn it, because I've been married for almost ten years. Just find somebody who was here when I was brought in; they'll tell you Carol was with me. She had to be."

"You were brought in by ambulance," Dr. Ordway said. "Alone."

"Oh, really? I suppose your ambulances always cruise up and down the beach at twelve-thirty in the morning looking for fares." The things they were telling Harry made no sense, and he wanted them to stop.

"The resort has its own beach patrol," the doctor continued. "You were found unconscious in front of cabin number four. We were notified, and dispatched an ambulance to pick you up. That's routine; we have a contract with the Tarawaulk management to handle all medical emergencies."

"Look," Harry said, trying to control his temper, "what you're saying about my wife is a lot of nonsense. I damn well ought to know whether or not I'm married. Just bring me a telephone and I'll call up the cottage and prove it to you."

"I don't think that would be advisable in your present condition."

"My condition would be a hell of a lot better if you'd let me talk to my wife!"

"I'm sorry."

Harry threw back the covers and started to get out of bed, but Ordway immediately grabbed his shoulders and forced him back down.

"Get your fucking hands off me."

"You've got to rest, Mr. Milford."

"That's the most important thing right now," Miss Styles chimed in.

"The only important thing is for me to get to a telephone."

"I'm afraid that's impossible," Ordway said.

"Wanna bet?" Harry grabbed Ordway's arms and pushed him away from the bed. The doctor's momentum carried him two or three steps backward, and he bumped into a chair, losing his balance. By now Harry was on his feet, and Miss Styles was rounding the foot of the bed in an effort to intercept him, but Harry had already broken into a run and moved out into the hallway just ahead of the doctor and nurse.

The linoleum was cold against his bare feet, and as he gained speed he heard somebody yell for an orderly. He came to a T in the corridor and arbitrarily turned left. Dead ahead was a closed door marked EXIT, but there was also a nurses' station at the next T with a strapping young orderly in a white lab coat positioning himself directly in Harry's line. Realizing he couldn't slow down or he'd be caught from behind, he closed the distance between himself and the orderly and decided what he was going to do.

Harry lowered his head as if he were going to run straight into the man, but at the last moment he slowed his pace slightly, faked right, then pushed off his right foot and threw his body to the left, glancing off the orderly, who had taken the fake and been drawn in the wrong direction.

Harry's knees touched the floor, but he was up and running in a second. A quick glance over his shoulder saw the orderly scramble to his feet and move out after him.

Like the other corridor, this one also had an exit at the end; only, there was no intersection from which someone could block his escape. Harry was running at top speed, but he could hear the orderly gaining on him, and a good fifteen yards still stood between him and the door. Suddenly the orderly dived into the air. For a moment his body hung parallel to the floor; then his outstretched hands slammed into the back of Harry's knees, and the two men crashed to the floor. Soon they were surrounded, and half a dozen people were tugging Harry to his feet. He put up a brief struggle, but it was useless. A wheelchair was brought over, and he slumped into it, the small crowd staring accusingly at him.

"Room two-twelve," Ordway said to the orderly. "And secure him with restraints."

"That's not necessary," Harry snapped. "You've made your point."

"I'll be the judge of that, Mr. Milford." He nodded to the

orderly, who pushed the wheelchair silently down the corridor.

"Friendly group of people you have around here," he said to the orderly after they'd left the others behind.

"You're the one who tried to escape. What did you expect?"

"Escape? I thought this was a clinic, not a prison."

"It's whatever you want to make it. Things can be very nice here if you have the right attitude."

"Listen, what's your name?" Harry asked.

"Ron."

"Well, Ron, supposing my attitude changed; do you think you could help me with a few things?"

"Like what?"

"Like getting a telephone in my room. That's very important to me."

"I don't have the authority to make decisions like that."

"No, but you could put in a good word with Ordway and the nurses. Tell them I realize I made a mistake and I'm ready to cooperate."

"And are you?" They came to a stop in front of the open door of Harry's room.

"Look, I want to get out of here as soon as possible. You can understand that. So I'm willing to play by their rules. Okay?"

The orderly pivoted the wheelchair, and they entered the room. "I'll see what I can do."

Harry climbed into bed. Immediately the young man began to fasten the leg restraints.

"You really don't need those," Harry said.

"If I leave them off, I'm out of a job." He tugged at a strap and fastened it with a buckle. "Is that too tight?"

"No, I guess not."

Harry stared at the ceiling while his arms were secured to the mattress, wondering how long he'd have to remain like this.

"Don't forget what I told you," he said as the orderly pushed the wheelchair out of the room.

"I'll remember, but I'm not making any promises."

Left alone and helpless, Harry fought off the panic that told him he'd never leave this place. People would begin to ask questions—his friends, the agency, and above all, Carol. But why were they lying about her? It must be some grotesque mix-up. It had to be. A man's wife just doesn't vanish with the sunrise. She'd been with him on the beach just before he'd blacked out. He remembered her touch and the comfort in her eyes. As soon as he could get his hands on a telephone, he'd get everything straightened out. Then he'd have her back, and feel safe, and together they could see this thing through.

He was beginning to feel a little better when he turned his head to look out the window for the first time, and what he saw shattered his short-lived sense of hope. He closed his eyes and thought back to that last moment of consciousness on the beach. His wife wasn't the only one he'd left behind at Tarawaulk Bay. There was also the dead body in cottage number nine. And they must think him responsible.

Still dulled by the conclusion he'd reached, he looked again at the sturdy iron bars that crisscrossed his window and proclaimed him a suspected murderer.

15

If they thought him a murderer, why didn't they come right out and say so? That was the question Harry kept turning over in his mind as he lay strapped to his bed, looking sometimes at the ceiling, sometimes at the barred window that was responsible for his theory. Perhaps, he reasoned, they were trying to force him to confess by keeping him in a kind of psychological isolation, by wrenching him out of contact with everything that was familiar to him. That would explain their denial of Carol. Yet, why would she agree to something like that? Of course, she might not know anything about it. If they'd sent her back to the cottage, she'd be sitting there right now waiting for a phone call telling her that her husband was conscious and she could see him.

"Shit," he said out loud, "that doesn't make any sense either." He clenched his fists in frustration. Even if they *had* sent Carol away to get some rest, she'd certainly be back by now, demanding to see him. So why wasn't she there?

Harry had no conception of time as he invented theory after theory, and discarded each one as flawed. The more possibilities he eliminated, the more resolved he became to find the right solution. He carefully reconstructed the events of the past days, from the beginnings of the nightmares and headaches to the first image flash as he stood in front of the office water cooler, right down to the moment Diane Kinney was killed and he collapsed in Carol's arms on the beach. He repeated the process several times, making sure he included every detail he could possibly recall; and each time, the same point stood out above all the rest, automatically forming the axis around which all the other pieces orbited. Convinced this was the ultimate question in his search, he spoke the words softly, giving them a reality of their own: "Who is Sutherland?"

The squeak of Miss Styles' rubber-soled shoes snapped Harry out of his contemplation. She carried a lunch tray, which she set on the movable stand that stood adjacent to his bed.

He hadn't really taken the time to look at her before, but now he saw that even in the utilitarian nurse uniform she was a most attractive young woman. Her figure was firm and shapely, her brown eyes soft and compassionate.

"Hungry?" she asked.

"Now that I think about it, yeah."

"Good. You have two choices." She lowered the stand and wheeled it over to where Harry could see it easily from his prone position. There was an appetizing salad dotted with bright-red cherry tomatoes, a small plate holding a roll and two pats of butter, an empty cup turned face-down on its saucer, and a steaming silver pot that he assumed contained coffee. To the back was a thick slice of apple pie, and in the middle of everything was a large plate with a plastic cover over it, which Miss Styles removed to reveal a steak, baked potato, and peas.

"The steak's rare; I can take it back if you don' t like it that way."

He wondered what the catch was. "You said I had two choices. What's the other one?"

"Intravenous feeding. It hardly compares, but it gets the job done."

"You're very persuasive."

"Not at all; it's entirely up to you. We don't like keeping those restraints on, any more than you do. So what's it going to be?"

"You can take them off. I don't particularly feel like getting tackled by Ron again."

"I'm glad to see you're a sensible man."

Reaching under the cloth napkin on the tray, she produced a capped hypodermic syringe and an alcohol swab.

"What's that for?"

"Just some vitamins."

He doubted that, but of course there was nothing he could do about it, and in a moment he felt the cold swab and the prick of the needle against his upper arm.

"There," she said as she recapped the syringe and put it in the pocket of her white uniform. "Now, suppose we get you ready for lunch?"

He watched in silence as she unfastened the restraints, and then there was the whir of the electric motor as she raised his bed to a sitting position.

Harry massaged his arms while she adjusted the movable stand and wheeled his lunch in front of him.

"There you go, Mr. Milford. Comfortable?"

"Fine."

"If there's anything you need, just press this." She held up an electric buzzer that was fastened to the side of his mattress with a safety pin.

"And you'll come running?"

"Somebody will."

"But I'd rather have you." He knew he was taking a chance, but he needed to make some friends around there.

"That's very nice," she said. "Thank you."

"You deserve it."

"Eat your lunch before it gets cold. I'll be back for the tray later."

She turned to leave, and he couldn't help noticing that she moved awfully well beneath the close-fitting uniform.

"Miss Styles?" he called after her.

She stopped and looked at him. "Yes?"

"Do you have a first name?"

"Kathy."

"I like that; it's right for you."

"I'm glad you approve." Though her tone was encouraging, he knew she was probably humoring him. Still, he had nothing to lose.

"How long am I going to be here, Kathy?"

"I don't know. Dr. Ordway wants to do some tests."

"Like what?"

"He hasn't said."

"But you could find out."

"Well, sooner or later he'll leave instructions at the nursing station."

"Listen, Kathy, I'll be honest with you; I need a friend, someone I can trust."

"Everybody here is interested in your welfare."

"That's not what I mean; you know that."

"Do I?"

"Look, put yourself in my place. I went for a walk on the beach and passed out. The next thing I know, here I am—strapped to a bed and surrounded by a building full of strangers. How would you feel if you woke up to something like that?"

"Scared."

"And that's just what I am. So help me."

"To do what?"

"To find out how I got here and what they plan to do with me."

"We told you how you got here."

"I don't believe it. I'm not going to jump out of bed and try to run out of here again, because I know it's useless. But I'm telling you that I was with my wife last night. Now, either Ordway or somebody above him is forcibly keeping Carol away from here, or for some reason she's cooperating with them. And I want to find out why."

"You're serious, aren't you?"

"Absolutely."

"I can't believe the doctor would be a party to anything like that." Her voice was no longer confident.

"You don't have to. Just don't disbelieve it. If I'm wrong, then it's my problem."

"And if you're right?"

"Then at least we know where we stand. Think about it, okay?"

She gave an almost imperceptible nod of her head.

"Good girl. There's just one more thing. If you decide to help me, I need to know everything you can find out about a man named Sutherland. I haven't the slightest idea who he is or what he does, but right now he's the most important person in my life."

"Your lunch is getting cold," she said, and left the room.

Harry cut into his steak, and red juice flowed out onto the plate. It was tender and done just the way he liked it. He ate everything in an effort to keep up his strength for whatever lay ahead. While he ate, he thought about what he'd said to Kathy. It was a calculated risk; there was no question about that, but what else could he do? Even if she went straight to Ordway and told him everything, what would happen? They'd probably use the restraints again, but he was already a prisoner, and completely at their mercy. Whether he had the freedom to get out of bed was of little consequence. So it was a good gamble. If he lost, he lost little, and if he won, he'd be on his way to finding out who Sutherland was and what, if anything, they'd done to Carol.

By the time he finished his lunch, he was getting a little drowsy. He thought about lowering the bed but decided against it. Kathy had said she'd be back for the tray, and he was anxious to see her, because if she were still vacillating, he wanted another opportunity to get her on his side. Yet, he couldn't help wondering how much he'd have to reveal to convince her, if he could convince her at all.

He was weighing the question when Ron, the orderly, came in carrying a telephone in one hand and a newspaper in the other. Harry looked at him with more than mild surprise.

"Enjoy your lunch?" Ron asked.

"It was very good."

"They got a new cook a couple of weeks ago. Big improvement over the last guy. I'll take the tray away as soon as I plug the phone in."

He reached behind the nightstand, slipped the four-pronged

plug into the circular jack, and set the phone down so that it was angled toward Harry. Then he picked up the receiver to make sure there was a dial tone.

"Works okay," Ron said as he hung up. "Dial nine first for an outside line. The newspaper's a bonus." He'd placed it on the movable stand next to the lunch tray.

"I hadn't expected such quick action," Harry said.

"Neither had I."

"I want you to know I really appreciate it."

"As a matter of fact, I had nothing to do with it."

"Oh?"

"That's right. This is all courtesy of Miss Styles. Apparently she buttonholed Dr. Ordway and went to bat for you. You must have done quite a number on her."

Ron reached down and picked up the lunch tray.

"And you don't approve," Harry said.

"It's not my business to worry about things like that."

"You don't have to be polite. What changed your mind?"

"I never had it made up."

"But you do now, and you don't think I can be trusted."

"That's right. I don't think you're ready for privileges yet."

"What's so privileged about being able to use a telephone and read a newspaper? Don't all the other patients have those things?"

"Not in this wing," Ron said.

The meaning slowly seeped into Harry, but he still had to ask the question.

"What exactly *is* this wing, Ron?"

"You mean they haven't told you?"

"I never asked. Now I am."

A look of smug satisfaction crossed the orderly's face. "It's the psychiatric wing," he said, and left without waiting for a reply.

When Ron was gone, Harry looked at the window. Now the iron bars had an explanation, and it occurred to him that it was somehow better to be suspected of murder than to be suspected of insanity.

Refusing himself pity, he turned his attention to the newspaper, searching it for any mention of the discovery of Diane Kinney's body. He turned page after page, wading through the boldface captions that announced strikes, riots, bombings, muggings—all the joys of modern civilization. In the midst of such a pathetic recitation he felt sure that the death of a beautiful young woman in the peaceful surroundings of Tarawaulk Bay would be a newsworthy item, but he found nothing, and that disturbed him. Then he looked at the dateline on the front page; it was a morning edition, which meant that it had gone to press shortly after the murder took place. That explained the omission. The body probably wouldn't even be found until some hapless maid received no answer to her knock on the door and let herself in with a passkey. Perhaps even as he sat in bed the grisly vignette was unfolding. He could picture it all quite clearly: the door opening a few inches, the called "Hello?" to make sure the cottage was empty, then the door swinging wide in front of the maid, and her attempt—perhaps unsuccessful—to suppress her gag reflex as she viewed the scene on the living-room floor.

But wait a minute, Harry thought. I never shut the door when I ran out of there. Not that he'd had the presence of mind to consider it, but even if he had, it would have meant his rearranging the body to allow for the arc of the door. That was something he was certain he could have never brought himself to do, which meant that sunrise would have found things just as he'd left them, and the body would have been discovered hours ago.

Unwillingly, he looked at the telephone that sat facing him on the nightstand. Though he'd demanded it earlier, now that it was there it presented a unique problem. Truth. Because no matter how frustrating it was for him to lie in bed and theorize, it carried the advantage of ignorance. If he didn't like the way one scenario was working out, he could always find a reason to discard it and move on to another that was more palatable. But the telephone wouldn't permit that; it would give him hard, cold answers to his questions, answers he might not like. Still, it had to be done.

He picked up the receiver, dialed nine for an outside line, and waited for the tone to click in. When it came, he dialed information and got the number for the main lodge at Tarawaulk Bay. Then he pressed the disconnect button and made his call. It was answered on the second ring.

"Thank you for calling Tarawaulk Bay. May I help you?" The woman's voice was pleasant, and for a moment Harry felt as if everything were going to be all right.

"Yes, I'd like to speak to Mrs. Milford in cottage number four," he said.

"Number four? One moment, please, and I'll connect you."

The seconds ticked by, and Harry braced himself for the sound of Carol's voice.

"Sir?" The woman was back on the line. "You did say cottage number four, didn't you?"

"That's right. Milford is the name; Carol Milford."

"I'm sorry, but that cottage is vacant, and we show no one by that name registered here."

"That's impossible. I'm Harry Milford. My wife and I checked in just yesterday."

"Perhaps I'd better let you speak to the manager."

Before Harry could reply, he was put on hold. The drowsiness that had come after lunch was getting worse, and he stifled a yawn. Then the line came alive again.

"Hello? Mr. Prescott speaking. Can I help you?"

Good. Prescott was the one on duty when he and Carol had arrived.

"This is Harry Milford, Mr. Prescott. My wife and I took cottage number four yesterday. I'd like to speak to her."

"There must be some mistake, Mr. Milford. That cottage has been vacant for several days."

"You're the one who's making the mistake. I ought to know where my wife and I are staying. In fact, you were the one who registered us. Don't you remember?"

"I pride myself on my memory, sir, and I didn't register you in cottage number four or anywhere else at the Bay."

"We were there, I tell you! Now, let me talk to my wife!"

"I see no reason to carry this conversation any further, Mr. Milford."

"Wait a minute; don't hang up." Sleep was rapidly overtaking Harry, and he had to fight to collect his thoughts, but an idea had occurred to him. "Let me talk to Diane Kinney in cottage number nine."

There was a slight pause before Prescott made his reply. "I'm afraid that's impossible."

You're damn right it is, Harry said to himself. "Oh? Why is that?"

"Because she checked out early this morning. I handled it myself."

"Really? Do you double as the coroner over there?"

"I beg your pardon?"

"You're a lousy liar, Prescott. And when I find Sutherland, I'll be sure and pass that on to him."

Harry slammed down the phone in disgust. He could no longer keep his eyes open, and as he laid his head against the pillow, he tried to think why he should be so sleepy. Then he knew. The injection Kathy had given him had been anything but vitamins.

He struggled to keep his mind working. Who could this Sutherland be, that he had the power to separate a man from his wife and make a murder appear as if it had never happened? But his question remained unanswered. In a matter of seconds he was asleep and plunged immediately into the nightmare.

16

There was no continuity to the dream this time. The image flashes that had littered his waking hours were mingled with disconnected scenes of his flight from the faceless pursuers who dogged him along the beach, one segment sometimes bleeding into another. Though he was deeply immersed in that dark section of his mind that was struggling to break into the present, Harry no longer felt any fear, because while he was firmly wed to those events that were invading his sleep, he was for the first time able to step back and view the spectacle as a dispassionate observer.

He saw himself running in the sand, felt his lungs aching for air, and experienced again the pain of his foot slamming into the rock and casting him helpless onto the beach. Stoically, he began his impotent attempt at escape, the spectator in him knowing full well what the results would be. Then, as was always the case, they encircled him, and he looked up, ready to see the shadowy blotches that hid their identities.

Harry drew a quick breath at what he saw. This time two of his pursuers had faces: the faces of Dr. Ordway and Ron, the orderly. They stood, as the others, with their arms folded across their chests, looking down at their captive with what seemed to be a mixed expression of admiration and annoyance. Then the high-pitched screech yanked Harry back to the present.

The sound continued, and it took him a few seconds to realize that he was no longer dreaming. He threw back the covers and walked to the window, the screech repeating at random intervals. The thrill of discovery was muted, though, because he'd known the source of the sound before his feet had touched the floor. It had clicked into place with unquestionable certainty, and his trip to the window to validate it with his eyes was a mere formality.

Yes, there it was—or they, to be precise—the commonplace that had eluded him for so long: seagulls. He gave an ironic chuckle as he watched them trace their graceful patterns over the Atlantic, their shrill cries piercing the air just as they had pierced his nightmare on so many occasions. Why hadn't he recognized it up until now? The answer came back with embarrassing swiftness. The dream had begun while he was still in Maryland; little chance of a gull giving him a clue there. As for the short time he'd spent at Tarawaulk Bay, the sound was an expected part of the background, plus the fact that he'd been too occupied with trying to discover what Carol had been hiding from him, and then with the sudden appearance of Diane Kinney. There hadn't been time to focus on anything else. But now it was out in the open; another piece of the puzzle had slid into place, and the bare outlines of a picture were beginning to take shape.

Still tired from the sedative, Harry leaned on the windowsill and tried to put his thoughts in order. He was in a contest against himself, and it didn't take him long to realize that the information he possessed was frustratingly sketchy. In fact, even the little he did know really couldn't qualify as anything more than a theory, and yet he had to make a start somewhere; it was either that or go on forever doubting himself until he was somehow magically presented with incontrovertible evidence. So, okay, he said to himself, what have you got? Put it together and see if it makes any sense.

It proved to be a painfully quick procedure. All he knew, or thought he knew, was that at some point in his past he'd been chased along a beach—possibly the one outside his barred window—and had been tripped up by a jagged rock sticking out of the sand. The tiny scar on the inside of his left ankle was the premise that supported his reasoning; that *had* to be where it came from; he couldn't let himself believe anything else. But beyond that, his knowledge tapered off rapidly. The panel of lights with its glowing number twenty-two *might* be connected with an elevator. Ordway and Ron *might* have been two of his pursuers on the beach, but they could easily have appeared in his dream simply because they were two people he didn't trust. And what about the bells in the tower, the computer-tape reels, and the fountain? He still had no explanation for those, not to mention the identities of Sutherland and J. McNeal, and the reason behind Diane Kinney's murder.

Harry felt more than a little angry with himself; he was making progress at a snail's pace. His only sources of information were the nightmare and the image flashes, and when they'd cast up their next clue was anybody's guess.

"Hello, there."

Startled, he turned from the window to see Kathy Styles standing just inside the doorway.

"Lovely view, isn't it?"

"If you don't mind looking through bars," he said.

"Can you spare a few minutes to talk?"

"I'm not exactly on a tight schedule. Come on in."

She walked across the room and stood next to him in front of the window.

"Would you rather lie down?" she asked. "You must still be a little weak."

"You mean from those 'vitamins' you gave me?"

"I don't prescribe the medication around here, Mr. Milford."

"You just do as you're told."

"A little more than that. I wasn't told to come in here and talk to you. But maybe I'm wasting my time."

"I'm sorry. I guess I just need someone to blame for this mess."

"I understand."

"Ron told me you were responsible for my telephone and newspaper. Thanks for your help."

"I didn't do that lightly; there was a very specific reason behind it."

"For instance?"

"How would you react if I told you I found out that Dr. Ordway has been lying to you?"

"It wouldn't surprise me in the least."

"Well, it surprised me. I've listened to the stories of a lot of patients in this wing, but the things you told me before lunch kept nagging at me. So I managed to get a look at your personal effects, and that's when I saw your driver's license: it lists you as a married man."

"It's nice to know someone believes me."

"Dr. Ordway was the one who'd briefed me on your background. I had no reason to doubt him, until now."

"I suppose that was quite a shock to you."

"Wouldn't it be to you? If someone you trusted turned out to be a liar?"

Harry couldn't help but think back to Carol's mysterious phone call to Washington, and whether or not her explanation was to be believed. "Yeah," he said, "I know the feeling. Now, the question is, what do we do about it?"

"That's what I want to talk to you about."

"Okay. Fire away."

"I'm going to help you get out of here."

"Why?" He spoke the question more with defiance than thanks.

"I told you; Dr. Ordway lied about you."

"And so you're going to throw open the doors to my cage and let me walk away."

"I don't happen to feel you belong in a cage, but if you want to stay here and see what happens, that's perfectly all right with me. I didn't come here to be ridiculed, so if you don't want my help, just speak up."

He hadn't the slightest idea whether or not he could trust her, but antagonizing a potential ally would certainly do him no good.

"I do want your help, Kathy; I want it very much. What I

don't want is to be set up to prove myself crazy, or whatever the hell they're trying to do to me. Now, that doesn't mean I'm accusing you of anything; it just means that I have to be convinced."

"All right, then, I'll convince you. When you first talked to me, you mentioned someone named Sutherland."

"Do you know who he is?"

"No, but Dr. Ordway seems to."

"What makes you think that?"

"I was attending a patient; the door to the room was partially open, and they were standing outside in the hall."

"Wait a minute," Harry interrupted. "Who are 'they'?"

"Dr. Ordway and Dr. Massey—he's chief of staff. Anyway, I'm sure they didn't realize I was around or they wouldn't have been so free with their conversation. As it was, I only got bits and pieces of what they were saying, but I distinctly heard the name Sutherland mentioned."

"By which one?"

"I couldn't tell, but it was obvious they both knew who he was."

"Did they mention me?"

"No, but I caught another name—someone I'd never heard of. McNeal. Does that mean anything to you?"

"McNeal," Harry said slowly. "It sure does."

"Who is he?"

"I don't know. In fact, he could very easily be a she."

Kathy looked at him quizzically.

"Don't ask me to explain," he said. "Just trust me."

"If I didn't trust you, I wouldn't be telling you any of this. But it's a two-way street, and all you've done so far is ask me questions."

"And I'm going to ask you one more: how do I get out of here?"

"So I've convinced you?"

"I have no choice."

"That's not exactly the answer I'd hoped for."

"Under the circumstances, it's the best I can do. We'll just have to assume we're not lying to each other. And until it's all over, we'll never really know."

"Then why should I do anything to help you?"

"Because if I'm telling the truth, they might have a lot more in store for me besides phony vitamin injections."

"And if you're not? What then?"

Harry shrugged. "Then you've let a raving lunatic with a king-sized persecution complex walk out the front door."

Kathy smiled at his frankness. "You have a marvelous way of resolving a person's doubts."

"I do my best. So choose your side."

She put her hands in the pockets of her uniform and stepped a few paces away. Then she turned and faced him.

"I already have, Harry." She'd never before called him by his first name.

"I'm supposed to give you another sedative with your dinner this evening," she said.

"But you won't."

"You're awfully sure of yourself."

"I have to be. Am I right?"

"Yes, you're right," Kathy said.

"Good."

"That remains to be seen."

"This is no time for second thoughts. Now, how do we go about getting me out of this place?"

She looked him straight in the eye and answered, "I don't know."

"That's terrific."

"Look, it's going to take time. You've already tried to escape once; that's not going to make it any easier, you know."

"So what do you suggest I do?"

"Wait."

"I could wind up dead waiting around here."

"Stop it. They'd never do anything like that."

"They've taken my wife from me. Who's to say they wouldn't take my life?"

Voices were heard in the hallway.

"I'll see you at dinner," Kathy whispered. "And don't worry; I'll think of something." She put her finger to her lips as a sign for him to keep quiet, and left Harry standing there, a helpless marionette who had just placed himself in the hands of an untested puppet master.

17

Shortly after Kathy left, Dr. Ordway stopped in to see Harry. He stood beside the bed and took his pulse, and to any other observer he would have certainly fit the mold of the dedicated physician.

"I was glad to hear that you decided to cooperate with us, Mr. Milford. As you can see, it has its advantages." Ordway looked casually toward the telephone.

There were any number of things Harry wanted to say. Instead, he forced out the expected reply. "I'm sorry for the trouble I caused you earlier. I was frightened."

"That's to be expected. But you trust us now, don't you?"

"Yes."

"Good. And you've given up that delusion about having a wife?"

The rules of the game were infuriating, but he knew he'd better tell Ordway what he wanted to hear.

"That was a long time ago," Harry said. "I'm single now."

"I see."

"You don't sound very convinced."

"You're the one who has to be convinced, Mr. Milford, not I."

"How soon before I can get out of here?"

"Not for a while yet, I'm afraid. We still have those tests I mentioned."

"When are you going to start them?"

"Tomorrow morning. Then, in two or three days we should know quite a bit more about you."

"You mean like whether or not I'm losing my mind."
"What makes you say that?"
"Because this is the psychiatric wing."
Ordway frowned. "Did someone tell you that?"
"What difference does it make? It's the truth, isn't it?"
"Yes, it is."
"Then you must think that I'm going insane."
" 'Insane' is a poor choice of words. I think that perhaps you're disturbed about something; I'd like to find out what it is so that I can help you with it. Is there anything you'd like to tell me?"
Go fuck yourself, Harry thought; who do you think you're kidding with your soap-opera bedside manner?
"I've been under a lot of pressure lately," he said to Ordway. "I came to Tarawaulk Bay to relax, and I guess it just all caught up with me."
"Are you happy in your work?"
"Are you?"
"Most of the time," Ordway replied.
"But not always."
"We all have our frustrations, certain areas of our lives that remain unresolved."
"Then you have just as much cause to be in this bed as I do."
His statement seemed to strike a nerve, and for a moment he had the feeling that Ordway might chuck all this nonsense and tell him what the hell was going on. Instead, the doctor continued to play his role. "That's a very interesting comment, Mr. Milford. We'll talk about it some more on my next visit. In the meantime, get some rest."
Once again, Harry was left alone.

The remainder of the afternoon passed slowly. He drifted in and out of short, restless naps, and neither the dream nor the image flashes yielded any new information. Then, about five o'clock, dinner came—but not with Kathy. It was Ron who entered the room carrying the tray crowded with plates of food.

Harry tensed at the sight of the orderly, wondering what he was going to do if Ron tried to administer a sedative.

"What's on the menu?" he asked as his bed was raised to a sitting position.

"Broiled lamb chops, mint jelly, the works."

"Sounds good."

"I suppose," the orderly replied. He uncovered a steaming plate containing two double-thick lamb chops, scalloped potatoes, and asparagus with hollandaise.

"Do you always bring dinner?"

"Why? What difference does it make?"

"I'm one of those people who needs a routine. I like to know what to expect from day to day."

"What you're really saying is that you'd rather have Miss Styles."

"Well, for one thing, she's a lot prettier than you. Of course, I'm sure she doesn't tackle runaway patients nearly as well."

Ron didn't laugh. "She's tied up with an emergency right now."

"Oh? What happened?"

"Freak accident. A guy stuck his hand out to make a left turn, and a car coming the other way sideswiped him—took it right off at the shoulder."

Harry looked at the meat on his plate and tried not to gag.

"Enjoy your dinner," Ron said, and left the room.

Harry took several deep breaths in an effort to settle his stomach, and though the nausea finally subsided, his appetite was gone. Pouring himself a cup of hot coffee, he tried to resolve this new turn of events and decided that Ron had been telling the truth. If Ordway had been at all suspicious of Kathy, he'd have simply sent another nurse to administer the evening sedative, and there would have been nothing that Harry could have done about it, because the padded restraints still hung loosely from the sides of his bed, waiting to be put to use at the slightest provocation. So Kathy was undoubtedly busy with the amputee, and she'd probably come by to pick up Harry's dinner tray in about a half-hour, under instructions to give him his sedative, but instead offering her plan of escape. That's what he wanted to believe. That's what he *had* to believe, and so he did.

Raising his cup with his right hand, he blew gently on the coffee and was just about to take a sip when a young nurse entered the room. The first thing Harry noticed was that she was carrying a hypodermic syringe.

"Mr. Milford?" she asked cheerfully as she approached his bed.

Harry set down his cup of coffee and didn't answer.

"This won't take a minute," she continued, "and then you can get back to your dinner." Quickly and efficiently she checked the plastic ID bracelet on his wrist and began to swab his arm with alcohol.

Harry was a jumble of indecision. He could refuse the injection, even get physical with the nurse, but ultimately that would do him no good. He had no choice but to accept the medication and hope for the best.

He felt the prick of the needle, and then it was over.

"There," the nurse said matter-of-factly, "that's that. Sorry for the interruption."

When she was gone, he picked up his coffee. It tasted good, and its warmth was a welcome comfort. Perhaps if he drank it all and kept his mind active, he might be able to overcome the sedative enough to carry out Kathy's plan. He took another sip and started to return the cup to its saucer, but in midmotion his arm became a useless object. His fingers lost all control, and the cup clattered to the tray, spilling the hot coffee across his dinner. Though there was no noticeable change in appearance, his limb felt as if it were swelling to the point where it would burst. In a matter of seconds it was an unbearable weight that dropped unceremoniously into the lamb and asparagus. The swelling sensation moved quickly down his left arm and both legs, and at the same time a tightness began to spread across his chest. Little by little he inched his left hand toward the call buzzer that was pinned to the side of the mattress. The pressure on his chest increased more and more; his facial muscles sagged, and his mouth went dry. Calling for help was a physical impossibility. Finally his hand was near the buzzer, and he was able to put the slightest pressure on it—but it was enough. His ears strained for the sounds of help, and soon he heard someone moving quickly toward his room. By sheer force of will he was able to turn his head in the direction of the doorway.

Ron walked quietly to the side of Harry's bed and looked down at the pitiful figure. Then he folded his arms across his chest in the same gesture of finality that the pursuers had used in the nightmare.

Harry's throat began to close. He wanted to open his mouth to take in more breath, but he couldn't. His chest felt as if it were about to cave in, and as his paralyzed eyes stared up at Ron, Harry knew with absolute certainty that he was about to die.

18

"This man is dead." Dr. Ordway pronounced the words with a noticeable lack of emotion and consulted his watch to fix the time of death. A young nurse disconnected the portable respirator that had been wheeled into Harry's room and dutifully pulled the top portion of the bed sheet over the corpse's face.

"Can you take him downstairs, or shall I get someone else?" Ordway asked Ron.

"No, I'll do it."

The brakes were removed from the wheels of the lightweight bed, and Ron maneuvered his cargo through the open door of the room and down the hallway toward an elevator. As he passed the nurses' station, muted conversations came to an abrupt halt. A few steps later, the orderly swung the bed around so that it wasn't blocking the corridor and pressed the elevator call button. The doors slid open; Ron wheeled the bed inside, and they began their descent to the basement. It was a short trip, and soon he was pushing the bed down an unpainted, concrete-walled corridor, at the end of which stood two swinging doors—the entrance to the morgue.

Ron winced as the bed banged its way into the room, and he looked down at the covered body as if half-expecting it to protest the rough treatment.

In keeping with its purpose, the morgue was a spartan area. Three walls were tiled in white from floor to ceiling; the fourth contained the roll-out, refrigerated cubicles where the bodies were stored. The faces of these cubicles were olive green, which gave them the appearance of oversized filing cabinets rather than receptacles of death. The autopsy table was in the far corner of the room, partitioned off with glass. A varnished table of blond wood stood next to one of the partitions, holding a typewriter and miscellaneous objects.

Ron went to the typewriter and inserted a blank tag into the machine. On it he typed Harry's name—last name first, Christian name, middle initial; under that the date of death; and finally the cause of death—respiratory failure. He then slipped a precut string through a hole at the end of the tag and walked over to Harry's body. Pulling the sheet up at the base of the bed, he tied the tag to the big toe of the left foot. Then he slid out an unmarked cubicle and transferred the corpse. Though he should have asked for help, he preferred to do the task himself.

Returning once more to the wooden table, he typed Harry's name on a small rectangular card.

The refrigerated cubicle slid into the wall, and Ron inserted the rectangular card into the identification window on its face.

He banged through the swinging doors with the empty bed and walked briskly toward the elevator at the end of the hall.

19

Kathy inched the door open hesitantly, then stepped inside the morgue. Since it was located in a little-traveled section of the building, she had been relatively certain that there would be no one else there, and she'd been right. She walked quickly to the wall of refrigerated cubicles and scanned the rows until she found the one with Harry's name. Gripping the handle firmly, she pulled; the cubicle slid effortlessly from the wall, bearing its contents under cover of the customary white sheet.

Working with practiced speed, Kathy prepared a hypodermic syringe, pulled the sheet down to Harry's waist, and injected the solution into his right arm. Then she took his chilled wrist in her hand and waited for the faint pressure of a pulse to register against her thumb.

Within seconds the artery began to throb with a light, irregular rhythm. She measured the beats against the sweep-second hand of her watch. As the pulse gradually grew in strength she became alert for other signs of life. Then, with the lazy movement of someone waking from a drugged sleep, Harry opened his eyes.

For a moment his mind was a blank, but Kathy's smiling face soon brought recognition, and his first sensation was of being terribly cold.

"Welcome back," she said.

"What happened to me?" The words rasped out of his throat.

"We'll talk about that later. Do you think you can sit up?"

It was only then that Harry realized he wasn't in a bed. With Kathy's help he rose to a sitting position.

"Jesus, I'm cold."

"You should be. This is the morgue, Harry. They tried to kill you."

He looked around the room, then at the drawerlike cubicle that held him. "How long have I been here?"

"Only about twenty minutes. If I had come down immediately, it would have looked suspicious."

"And in the meantime, I might have frozen to death."

"But you didn't."

"Lady, you've got some questions to answer."

"Let's get you out of there, and I'll explain."

She helped him climb down from the cubicle, closed it, and led him across the room to the autopsy area, where she drew the curtains over the glass partitions so the two of them would be effectively shielded from anyone who might enter the room.

"Okay," he said, "let's hear it."

"When I left you this afternoon, I didn't have any idea how I was going to get you out of here; as it turned out, Dr. Ordway solved my problem for me. About ten minutes before I was due to deliver your dinner tray, he stopped by the nurses' station and told me he was going to change your medication and that he'd personally prepare the hypodermic. The whole thing struck me as odd—especially when he insisted on preparing the hypo; there was no reason for that."

"So how did you stop him?"

"I didn't. I couldn't very well contradict a doctor's orders; so I just went on with my routine. But as soon as he left the nurses' station, I checked your chart to see what the new medication was."

"And that's when you discovered they wanted me dead."

"No. The entry on the chart was for a sedative very similar to the one I'd given you at lunch. I couldn't understand why he'd made the change, but a doctor doesn't have to justify his reasons to a nurse. It was when he came back from the dispensary with the hypo that I knew for sure something was wrong."

"How?"

"I was a pharmacist for two years before I decided to get my RN. The solution in the syringe was too cloudy to be the sedative Ordway had prescribed. Offhand, I could think of two or three drugs that looked like that—all of them lethal in that quantity."

Harry listened intently.

"The trays had arrived by then," she continued, "and that's always a busy time for the nurses—matching up evening medications with the right patients, double-checking special menus, that kind of thing. So as soon as Ordway was out of sight, I pretended to drop the hypo and break it. That gave me an excuse to go to the dispensary and make the switch."

"To what?"

"A powerful anesthetic that slows the body's vital functions to a bare minimum."

"That was taking one hell of a chance."

"I know. But if I hadn't done it, you'd be stone-cold dead right now."

"And where were you while I was being shot up with this stuff?"

"Answering a phony page. I suppose Ordway thought I might be on to him. He was right, of course."

"That still doesn't explain how I wound up in the morgue."

"Simple. He pronounced you dead."

"But I wasn't."

"As far as he was concerned, you'd been given a lethal dosage of medication. He had every reason to believe you were ninety percent gone by the time he got to you. All he had to do was go through the motions for a few minutes and then announce it was over. Since he was the only doctor present, who was going to question him?"

"So he had me put on ice to hurry things along."

"Right," Kathy said. "With what he thought was in your system, it would have been only a matter of minutes before the sudden drop in temperature completed the job for him."

Harry shook his head in wonder. Someone had actually tried to kill him. What did he know that was so threatening?

"I owe you my life, Kathy."

"I did what I could; I'm just glad it worked. Now it's time for us to leave."

"I can't ask you to come with me."

"You're not. I don't want to be around when they find out you're gone."

"Okay; how do we do it?"

"We're in the basement of the building; there's a fire exit that runs under the bluff and empties on the beach. Do you feel strong enough to walk?"

"In this?" He looked down at the loose-fitting hospital gown that draped his body.

"If your clothes have been sent down to storage, I'll bring them. Now, let's get going."

He waited behind the curtains in the autopsy area while she tentatively pushed open one of the swinging doors and checked the corridor. Then she motioned to him to come ahead. Still groggy, he crossed the room and followed her down a short section of hallway to a steel door marked FIRE EXIT.

"The tunnel's about fifty yards long, and well-lit," Kathy whispered. "And you'd better lose that white gown before you get to the beach, or you'll stand out like a light at this time of night."

"Wait a minute; I don't have anything on under this."

"I'm a nurse, Harry. I've seen hundreds of naked men. Now, once you're outside, keep low. I'll get the car and drive down to the frontage road. When you see my headlights blink, make your move."

"Are you sure it'll work?"

"No. Now, get going." She turned the knob and pushed

open the door. "See you on the beach." She gave him a gentle shove and closed the door behind him.

The tunnel was constructed of reinforced concrete with caged 150-watt light bulbs every twenty-five feet providing the overhead illumination. Even though it was a straight shot to the other end, red arrows were stenciled on the walls and floor to point the way out in case of panic. Harry glanced behind him once at the closed door, then moved silently toward freedom.

As he stood in front of the exit that opened onto the beach, he slipped out of the hospital gown. Naked, he pressed down on the metal crossbar, and the door swung open, admitting the cold night air. He took one deep breath and stepped outside.

The sand sifted between his toes, and he dropped immediately to his knees. Easing himself down on his stomach, he lay still and surveyed the scene in front of him.

The frontage road was a narrow two-lane strip of asphalt that bisected the shoreline and ran parallel to the ocean, leaving about twenty yards of beach on either side. The full moon glinted off the water, and the surf pounded in the background. As he lay there, tense and cold, waiting for the approaching sound of Kathy's car, another piece of the nightmare clicked into place: the pounding of the surf was the familiar but unidentifiable sound that had punctuated his flight along the beach. Like the seagulls, it had been too obvious to recognize until it had been isolated from the other aspects of the dream. But now he was sure of it.

The sound of the car grew gradually louder, and he could see it approaching, moving steadily along the road with its headlights turned off. Then it stopped at a ten-degree angle to his left, and the lights blinked once.

Harry hesitated, then got to his feet and began to sprint across the beach to the car. The aftereffects of the anesthetic made it difficult for him to keep in a straight line, but he pushed on. As he ran, he noticed jagged pieces of rock, uncovered by the evening breeze, sticking up through the sand.

He became convinced that this was the beach where he'd fallen in the nightmare.

Now that only a few strides separated him from Kathy's car, his body became charged with the challenge of the task that lay ahead: he had pieced together the main structure of the dream, and his instincts told him that he was on the way to learning the identity of Sutherland and McNeal, the reason behind Diane Kinney's death, and the meaning of the image flashes.

When he reached the car, Kathy leaned across the front seat and opened the door for him. He got in quickly, feeling a little dizzy from the effects of the sprint. She waited for him to catch his breath, and then he realized she was appraising his nakedness. Embarrassed, he dropped a hand to his lap.

"I thought you said you'd seen hundreds of naked men."

"That doesn't mean I have to stop looking." She was wearing a heavy wrap coat over her uniform, and her purse rested on the seat next to her.

"Just give me my clothes," Harry said.

"Clothes?"

"Come on, don't tell me you couldn't get them."

"I was in a hurry."

"Oh, Jesus. I can't ride around naked."

"Why not?"

"Because it's embarrassing, that's why!"

Kathy started to laugh, and couldn't help noticing that Harry's hand was having more and more to conceal. "Look in the back," she said.

He turned and saw what appeared to be a laundry bundle wrapped in brown paper, with his name on it. He lunged at it and ripped it open, his clothes spilling onto the back seat.

"Just my luck," she said. "Alone on the beach with a bare-assed man, and all he can think about is getting dressed." Then she put the car in gear and started off down the road. Harry began to relax back into his seat.

"Hey." Kathy honked the car and waved suddenly.

"What!" With a gasp, Harry twisted around just quickly

enough to catch sight of a white-coated man waving at them from the beach.

"That was Jack," said Kathy. "Don't worry. He knows it's about time for me to check out."

"But what if he saw me?" Harry squeaked. He was breathing in short gulps.

"He'll think you're just another naked man I picked up off the beach."

"Next time you feel the urge to do something like that, warn me, okay?"

"Don't worry, Harry," Kathy said, patting his knee with her free hand. "We'll make it."

Harry tried to breathe deeply, to calm himself. And even if they did make it, what then? He realized he would be facing the answers soon now.

20

Harry dressed in the cramped quarters of the front seat, then settled back to drink in his freedom. Up ahead, the frontage road merged with the main highway, and Kathy switched on the headlights. There were few cars on the multilane road, and the New England scenery slipped by them in the moonlight.

"Feel good to be back in the real world again?" she asked.

"I wish I knew what the real world was, but I guarantee you I'm going to find out."

"Harry, do you have any idea why they tried to kill you?"

"If I did, I'd have you drive to the nearest police station and tell them to come down on those bastards as hard as they could."

"Somehow, you must represent a terrible threat to them."

"The question is, why? I'll figure it out, though. I've come this far; I'll make it all the way to the end."

"Just so it isn't the end of your life."

"Let's hope not."

"I don't know what you're involved in," she said, "and apparently you don't either, but I think you should quit."

"I can't."

"Why not? What have you got to prove?"

"That I'm in charge of my own life."

"Is that so important?"

"To me it is. I'm Harry Milford; I've got a wife named Carol, a house in Maryland, and a desk job with the government. But somewhere along the line something went wrong. Things started falling apart, and I've got to find out why. A man's life just doesn't dissolve in front of his eyes. There has to be a reason, a rational explanation that winds up telling me I am who I know I am. I can't walk away from it, any more than I can walk away from myself."

She gave a sigh of resignation. "Okay; where do we go from here?"

"Now that I've got my wallet back, just drop me someplace where I can rent a car."

"No deal."

"Look, Kathy, I know I'd be dead now if it weren't for you, but there's no reason why you should get in this any deeper than you already are."

"You owe me, Harry, and I'm going to collect by riding this thing out with you."

"I don't even know what's waiting for me out there. I can't let you jeopardize your life."

"It's my life, god damn it, so stop being so stubborn and let me do what I want."

"All right. You can take me to my house in Maryland; but after that, I'm on my own."

"We'll worry about that when we get there."

"Now, Kathy—"

"Harry," she interrupted pleasantly, "shut up."

They were winding their way up a fairly steep grade when the quick blast from the siren startled them both and sent a stab of fear through Harry. Kathy immediately looked in the rearview mirror and saw the police car, its red lights flashing in the night. Apprehensively, she pulled onto the shoulder of the road.

"We're had," Harry said. He thought of Jack, on the beach near the clinic.

"Not necessarily. Just take it easy and let them make the first move."

The two officers approached them from either side of the car. Obediently, they rolled down their windows.

The policemen were young and lean, and the one on Kathy's side wore a neatly trimmed moustache. "Good evening," he said, raising his hand casually to the brim of his cap.

"What's the trouble, officer?" Kathy asked.

"We noticed your exhaust was a little heavy coming up the grade."

"Oh?"

"Nothing bad enough to warrant a citation, but you'd better have it looked at before it gets any worse."

"I certainly will. I had no idea it was smoking like that."

"May I see your driver's license, please?"

"Of course." She opened her purse, and there, on top of her wallet, was a snubnosed .38-caliber handgun. In an instant, the beams from the officers' flashlights were trained on the black metal of the gun.

"Don't worry; I have a permit for it," Kathy said casually.

"Would you both step out of the car?" The officer on Harry's side asked the question in a tone that left no room for argument.

The two policemen simultaneously opened the car doors, and though their attitude was still courteous, there was a definite air of efficient caution that hadn't been there before.

"I'll take your purse," the one with the moustache said to Kathy.

She handed it to him, and they followed the officers to their squad car, where Harry and Kathy were ushered into the back seat. Then the gun was removed and the purse returned.

"We'll need both your driver's licenses," the other policeman said. "And please take them out of your wallets."

They did as they were told, and while the moustached officer moved to the radio on the dashboard, the other kept his place beside Harry, who was trying his best to remain calm. Why hadn't Kathy told him about the gun? What if the clinic had discovered him missing and given his description to the police? Wait a minute, he told himself. All they could do was report a stolen corpse; otherwise, Ordway would have a hell of a lot of explaining to do.

Harry was in the middle of his private interrogation when the officer in the front seat ended his radio conversation and walked back to Kathy, holding out the gun, grip-first.

"Everything checks out—with you too, Mr. Milford." He leaned in and handed them their driver's licenses. "You're free to go now."

They got out of the squad car, and the officers slammed the doors shut.

"Sorry for the inconvenience," the clean-shaven one said, "but in a situation like this, we can't afford to take any chances."

Kathy brushed his apology aside. "No problem. There must be plenty of people carrying guns for reasons besides protection."

"That's for sure."

"Drive carefully, now," the moustached one said. "And don't forget to have that exhaust checked."

"I won't."

By the time she and Harry got back into their car, his hands were cold as ice and covered with sweat. The policemen gave a friendly wave as they drove past, and he returned it routinely.

"Jesus Christ," he said in exasperation, "you could have at least told me about the gun."

"I've been carrying it for over a year; it never crossed my mind."

"Terrific. Just what do you plan to do with it?"

"Shoot somebody, if I have to; I'm not afraid to use it."

"Expecting trouble?" he asked sarcastically.

"I bought it right after one of the nurses was raped in the clinic parking lot."

"Oh. I'm sorry."

"She would be, too, if she knew what happened to her."

"What do you mean?"

"The attacker beat her so badly that she suffered irreparable brain damage. She's been a vegetable ever since, and as far as anybody knows, the animal who did it is still running around loose."

Harry felt like a fool. "I stand corrected."

"Forget it," she said. Then the animation returned to her voice. "Listen, we'll be crossing the Maryland state line soon; do you want to drive?"

"Sure."

They got out of the car and exchanged places. Soon they were on their way again, the cadence of the S curves requiring all his concentration and forcing the incident of the gun from his mind.

21

When they crossed the state line into Maryland, Harry felt strangely alone. He looked over at Kathy, who was slouched down in the seat and sleeping peacefully. So here I am, he thought, an escaped "corpse" returning home—for what? A confrontation with Carol? A bullet in the head, like Diane Kinney? The options were hardly inspiring. In fact, it had crossed his mind more than once that it would be very easy just to keep driving, to leave Maryland behind him and his questions unanswered. But no matter how often he entertained the thought, he knew that ultimately he'd reject it. He was on a collision course with the truth, and the only thing he could do was brace himself for the impact.

Still asleep, Kathy shifted her position, and her purse tipped against Harry's thigh. It was as he reached down to move it that it occurred to him to steal the gun. At first he chuckled at the idea. The last time he'd stolen anything was when, at twelve, his adolescent curiosity had gotten the better of him and he'd lifted a girlie magazine from the newsrack of a large liquor store. Even then he'd left fifty cents amid the stacks in order to salve his conscience. But a gun? That was something else entirely. He hadn't even fired one since he was in the army, and then only on the occasions of mandatory target practice. In fact, as he remembered it, he'd been a lousy shot, inspiring his sergeant to new heights of obscenity. To steal Kathy's gun would be sheer foolishness. Yet, the purse continued to rest against his thigh, and he made no move to dislodge it.

All right, he asked himself sternly, suppose you had the gun? Would you be able to use it? Could you kill a person? Because that's what it would come down to, you know. You'd have no chance to aim for a leg or a shoulder; you'd miss a small target like that for sure. So you'd be firing point-blank into the torso—the chest area, probably, because stomach wounds can still allow an opponent to return your fire. Wasn't that what you were taught in the service? Let the bullet rip its hot path through the heart or lungs, maybe splintering a rib or two in the process. Could you do that, Harry? To Sutherland? Or McNeal? Or . . . Carol?

He hated himself for adding Carol's name to the list. He'd rather be dead than learn she was involved; but there was no question about the others. One, or both, had apparently been responsible for Ordway's attempt to kill him, and he'd be damned if he was going to give them another free chance.

It was settled, then: he'd take the gun. It was less than an hour's drive to his house, and once they arrived, he'd send Kathy on her way, and that would be that. With a little luck, she'd never notice it was missing until it was too late to do anything constructive about it.

Checking to make sure she was still asleep, he slid his hand carefully down the side of the purse and undid the clasp, muffling the metallic click as best he could. Slowly he spread the bag open until there was enough room to extract the gun without brushing against anything. Then, his hand lowering like a magnetic claw in an arcade game, he gripped the gun between his thumb and his index and middle fingers and began to raise it. Everything was going fine until a gold compact dislodged and clattered against a lipstick case. Harry froze, the gun half in and half out of the purse, expecting Kathy to wake up at any moment. But the seconds ticked by, and she slept on.

Once again he resumed his upward movement, until the gun hung suspended in the air above the car seat. With one smooth motion he drew the weapon across his stomach and tucked it in the waistband of his trousers, well behind his unbuttoned sport coat. Then he shut the purse as quietly as possible and placed his hand back on the steering wheel.

He'd done it. Now he was armed for the fight.

Fifteen minutes later Kathy awoke, bleary-eyed and not altogether refreshed.

"Hello, there. That was a nice little nap you had."

"Hello, yourself; that nice little nap gave me a stiff neck."

"I'm surprised. You seemed comfortable."

"Hey," she said, looking at the instrument cluster behind the wheel, "we better stop for some gas or we'll be thumbing it the rest of the way. Pull into the next Chevron station; I've got a credit card."

He looked at the fuel gauge and saw that it was dangerously close to the empty mark. Damn it! Why hadn't he noticed that before!

"Oaky," he said, "but I'll pay for the gas."

"Why should you?"

"Because I insist." His reply came out harsher than he'd wanted it to, but she just shrugged and tried to work the kink out of her neck. Relieved for the moment, Harry reached down and turned on the radio in an effort to avoid any more conversation.

Soon a blue-and-red Chevron insignia shone ahead of them down the highway.

"There's one," Kathy said. "We better take it."

Reluctantly he decelerated and pulled into the station. The office and service bays were brilliantly lit, and a tall, lanky red-haired attendant ambled over to their car.

"'Evening," he said to Harry. "Fill 'er up?"

"Right." Then he turned to Kathy. "What do you take?"

"Low-lead," she said across to the attendant.

He nodded and moved to the pump.

Kathy stretched and massaged the back of her neck. "I could stand a trip to the john." She reached for her purse, and Harry panicked.

"Are you sure you want to? It's probably filthy."

"So I'll close my eyes."

She grabbed the strap of her handbag and started to open the door.

"Why don't you at least leave your purse here?"

She looked at him, amused by what she took to be his awkward concern. "Relax, Harry; nothing's going to happen. Besides, I need my comb and brush; my hair must be a mess after that nap. I won't be long."

Kathy picked up the purse and got out of the car. As she walked across the asphalt toward the rest rooms, Harry sat tensely behind the wheel. If she didn't notice the lightness of her bag, she'd discover what he'd done when she opened it. And then what?

The attendant was drawing a rubber squeegee across the windshield, the dampness coming off the glass in neat, six-inch-wide paths. He grinned at Harry. Harry smiled weakly.

Suddenly Kathy halted, turned, and began walking quickly back toward the car. There was a look of mild urgency on her face, and Harry started to formulate a stumbling, inadequate explanation. When she got within hailing distance of the attendant, she stopped.

"Hey, Red," she called. "Check the oil and add a quart if it's low."

He raised a bony, freckled hand in response, and she was once again on her way to the rest room.

Two or three minutes later Harry paid the tab with his own credit card, being careful not to expose the gun when he removed his wallet. Shortly after that, Kathy returned to the car.

"Well," she said as she slid in and shut the door, "do I look like a woman again?"

"You look fine. Just great." Had she fixed her hair? It looked the same. She wore it in a loose, layered cut, and it was hard for him to tell. He wished he'd taken closer notice of it when she'd left the car.

"I paid for the gas," he said.

"You didn't have to do that, but thanks. Did it need any oil?"

"No; it was okay."

"That's a pleasant surprise. You ready to go?" She gave absolutely no indication of knowing anything about the stolen gun. Either she'd never opened her purse or she was planning to use the knowledge as leverage somewhere down the line.

"Hey," she said, "anything wrong?"

Harry realized he was staring at her. "Sorry. Just drifting." He switched on the ignition and pulled out onto the highway.

As he turned the corner onto his street, all the familiar sights felt alien to him. He slowed to a crawl, wanting to delay for as long as possible the moment when he'd pull up in front of his house. Every other time he'd driven down that street, he'd been happy he was going home. Now he dreaded it.

"Don't worry," Kathy said softly, "she'll be there."

"That's what I'm half-afraid of."

"I know. If you like, I'll come in with you."

"After I have a few minutes alone with her."

"Sure; I understand. But remember, they may very well have contacted her and told her that you're dead. So the sight of you standing on the front porch could be quite a shock."

Harry wasn't listening. He'd stopped the car and was looking past Kathy at his house.

"Holy Christ," he said in a hollow tone.

"Harry? What's the matter?"

"That's where I live."

She turned and looked out the window. There, jutting out of the lawn and plainly visible beneath the full moon, was a rectangular metal sign with a blazing red message for all to see: FOR SALE.

22

Stunned, Harry slammed the gearshift into park and got out of the car without bothering to switch off the ignition. His eyes fixed on the metal sign, he stepped up onto the sidewalk and stood like some bewildered time traveler suddenly popped into the middle of a Lewis Carroll landscape. For no reason other than to convince himself that what he was seeing was real, he walked over to the sign and lightly ran his fingertips across its slick, dew-covered surface. Then he raised his eyes to the address that angled across the brick chimney. There was no mistake. This was his house.

The sound of a car door closing registered vaguely in the back of his mind, and the next thing he knew, Kathy was standing beside him. With a gesture as uninhibited as if she'd been doing it for years, she slipped her arm under his and took hold of his hand, still moist from the dampness of the sign.

"Are you sure this is the place?" Her question was kindly put and almost rhetorical, yet it left room for a reply.

Harry turned to her with a look devoid of all emotion. "I know my own house." There was a dullness in his voice , the dullness that comes from an acceptance of defeat.

"This doesn't have to be the end," Kathy said.

"I didn't want her to be here . . . but not this way."

"What makes you think she isn't here? Just because the house is for sale doesn't mean she's vanished."

Harry began to come out of his fog. She was right. The sight of the sign had been such an unexpected blow, it had temporarily robbed him of the will to fight back.

"That was stupid of me. Of course she's here." As soon as he spoke the words, he felt better.

"But what if she's already gone to the hospital and they've discovered I'm missing?" he wondered aloud.

"Why don't we ring the doorbell and find out?"

He gave a weak smile. "Wait here."

Walking across the lawn, he tried to decide what he would say to Carol when she opened the door, then gave it up, realizing that the moment would take care of itself. He climbed the two steps that led to the porch and leaned once on the bell. The fact that there had been no lights showing from the front of the house hadn't disturbed him; Carol was a practical woman, and she often turned off the lights in an unoccupied room. So she could easily be in the den or their bedroom. Perhaps, if they *had* told her he was dead, she'd been crying and was now desperately trying to make herself presentable before answering the door. Satisfied with his explanation, he waited patiently.

No one came. The house remained dark and quiet. Again he pushed the bell, holding it longer this time, and it dawned on him that he wasn't hearing the familiar two-tone chime.

Disturbed, Harry thrust his hand into his coat pocket and felt his keys. He withdrew them and searched out the one to the front door. Not allowing himself any time to reconsider, he slid it into the lock and gave it a quick half-turn to the right. With a slight push the door opened a crack.

He removed the key, placed his hand firmly on the knob, and stepped inside. The house was pitch black, the drapes blocking out the moonlight. His free hand automatically moved for the light switch on the wall that illuminated the small entry hall. He flipped it on, and there was a split-second lag between the action and his comprehension that nothing had happened. The area was still dark.

He worked the switch back and forth several times, with no result, wanting to believe the cause was something as simple as a burned-out bulb.

"Carol?" The sound of his own voice seemed cold in the quiet darkness.

"Carol? It's me—Harry. Anybody home?"

His call was answered by the sound of dried leaves softly scuttling across the driveway.

There was something wrong, something besides the fact that Carol was apparently not at home. There could be any number of possible explanations for that. But this was Harry's house, and he'd been alone in it many times before. This time, something was not as it should be.

He began slowly to feel his way along the wall into the living room and toward a lamp. When he got to where he thought it should be, he groped with his hand in the darkness, and was met only by empty space. At first he thought he must have miscalculated, but the more he varied his position, the more convinced he became that there was nothing there.

Concerned, he made his way out the front door and jogged across the lawn to Kathy.

"What's wrong?" she asked. "Nobody home?"

"It doesn't look that way. Do you have a flashlight in the car?"

"Sure; but why?"

"I'll explain later. Where do you keep it?"

"In the glove compartment. It should be open."

In a few seconds he was back with the flashlight. He tested the beam and found it was strong.

"Wait here," Harry said.

"Uh-uh. I did that already. This time I'm coming with you."

"No way."

"Then give me back my flashlight."

"Don't be silly."

"You're the one who's being silly—insisting on going in there alone."

"You know, you're one hell of a stubborn woman."

"Thanks. Now, get going; I'm right behind you."

They reached the porch and stood for a moment in front of the open door; then Harry switched on the flashlight, and they stepped inside. He immediately turned in the direction of the living room. The beam of light illuminated the scene he knew he would find.

It was empty. Not a single piece of furniture remained.

Kathy brushed up against him, but she said nothing. Instead, she followed him into the kitchen. Like the living room, everything was gone. He trained the light on the area where the breakfast table had been and thought back to the night he and Carol had sat there while he tried to explain what was happening to him. Now it was a lifeless area, a half-struck stage setting. Routinely he reached for the wall switch. It didn't work—not that he'd really expected it to. But he had to try it, just as he had to walk silently from room to vacant room, knowing that he'd be met each time with another succession of barren walls and uncluttered expanses of carpet.

Finally they reached the master bedroom. He stepped inside, the flashlight shining haphazardly on a space of wall where an oil painting had once hung, a painting they had bought on impulse one windy Saturday afternoon. And now, like the whole of his married life, it was gone.

"They've pulled her away from me like she never existed."

"What did you expect?"

The impact of Kathy's words registered at the same moment that he felt the immobilizing pressure of her fingers at the base of his skull. In an instant her other hand reached beneath his coat and removed the gun from the waistband of his trousers, as if she'd known it was there all the time.

"My advice is not to move, Harry. Because I can put you out any second I choose." To emphasize her point, she increased the pressure slightly, and his vision began to cloud.

"Don't try to talk; just listen," she continued. "This is where I say good-bye. And just for the record, I don't enjoy doing this. But I have my orders, and one simply doesn't disobey Mr. Sutherland." Curiously enough, she spoke the last few words with a distinct British accent. Then her fingers bore down hard into Harry's flesh, and he was lost in a tide of swirling darkness.

23

Face down, Harry's unconscious form lay sprawled in the middle of the dark, vacant bedroom as if he were a forgotten fighter in an empty ring. His eyelids struggled open, and his first sensation was of the carpet pile pricking his face. The base of his skull tingled where Kathy's strong fingers had done their job so expertly. A sense of embarrassment passed through him; he'd let himself be taken in by someone he'd trusted. That he was a painfully naïve virgin in this fantastic game was all too obvious.

He shifted to a sitting position and took stock of his circumstances. For openers, he was alone again. Strangely enough, the more he thought about it, the more he liked it. At the very least, he wouldn't run the risk of waltzing into the enemy's arms like he'd done with Kathy.

The enemy. Sutherland and his people had managed to turn Harry's life into a battlefield and force him to conduct a one-man war. Needless to say, he didn't care much for the odds.

He massaged the back of his neck. Kathy was a well-trained professional. She could have easily killed him, but she hadn't. So they wanted him alive—for the time being, at least. And what about Ordway? Had he really intended to take Harry's life, or had it all been an intricate scheme to get him to trust Kathy?

He shook his head in despair. He was doing nothing but sliding deeper and deeper into a maze of unanswered questions. Perhaps the best thing would be to give up. He checked to see if he still had his wallet; he did. Taking it out, he flipped through the thick stack of credit cards, each in its own clear-plastic envelope. They were the magic beads of the late twentieth century, entitling their bearer to airline tickets, hotel rooms, food, clothing, automotive transportation, everything, in fact, that Harry would need to fade out of sight.

No; that would accomplish nothing. It was foolish to think he could escape Sutherland. Besides, he'd meant it when he told Kathy he had to prove he was in charge of his own life. Nobody had the right to manipulate another human being the way Sutherland was manipulating him.

Harry got to his feet; he thought he was feeling all right, but then, he'd been through so much lately that he'd forgotten what it was like to feel good. He saw the outline of the flashlight on the floor, picked it up, and switched it on. A quick survey of the area told him that the gun was gone. He wasn't surprised. They obviously wanted to keep him as helpless as possible, and they were doing a damn good job of it.

"All right," he said aloud to the empty room, "where do I go from here?" He'd been asking himself that a lot lately, and now the silence of his empty house mimicked the silence in his mind.

He couldn't just stand there and wait for something to happen. They were undoubtedly watching him and speculating on what his next move would be—waiting to see whether he'd give up. But he wasn't going to afford them that satisfaction. If they wanted him out of this game, they were going to have to put him out—for good.

He left the bedroom and made his way to the front door. He had an idea. Making sure the street was quiet, he put out the flashlight and walked across the front lawn to where the For Sale sign stood. It was easy to read in the moonlight, and he memorized the realtor's name and phone number. The first thing in the morning he'd call them up and see if they could give him any information on Carol. At least it was a start, and the way events had been overtaking him, he was sure the phone call would generate some kind of action.

He closed his eyes to test himself on the name and number, when the inside of his eyelids exploded in a flash of light and a scene stood before him, as if momentarily illuminated by a very bright flare. The image was clear and concise, but gone in an instant. What he had seen was himself standing in an elevator and pushing the button for the twenty-second floor.

Harry forced himself to keep his eyes closed, hoping the scene would reappear. It didn't, but another did. It was the image of the office door with the name J. McNeal on it; however, this time it was more inclusive and revealed the office number—2201. This was followed in quick succession by a third image flash—the familiar multicolored fountain. It too was a wider view than he'd seen in the past, and he could discern the outlines of a building behind it, though it was much too vague to allow any positive identification.

When nothing else happened for the next several seconds, he opened his eyes and considered what he'd just seen. The number on the office door and his riding in an elevator to the twenty-second floor confirmed each other. Now he realized that the initial flash of the light panel with the glowing number twenty-two that had been so terrifying at the Maryland agency was the forerunner of this information. As for the building behind the fountain, it was impossible for him to identify at the present, but he was willing to bet any amount of money that it contained J. McNeal's office.

He was ecstatic. His mind was functioning like the iris on a camera, gradually opening up wider and wider to take in more and more of the picture. He had no idea why this was happening. As far as he knew, he'd never met a J. McNeal, but if the process kept up, then sooner or later he was bound to arrive at the end of his maze, and he knew beyond the shadow of a doubt that when he got there, three people would be waiting for him: his wife, McNeal, and Sutherland.

Harry was charged and ready to go. The thought of spending hours or maybe even days before he got his next input of information was more than he could stand. He had to do something, to keep moving. He wanted to force the events to happen, to kick up the speed of the projector and race to the end of the film.

Then, as if it were the only logical step he could possibly take, he knew what he was going to do. Whether it would work or not was something else, but it was definitely worth a try. The worst it could generate would be a call to the police, but somehow he felt that Sutherland wouldn't let the police intervene, because if that's what he'd wanted, he'd already had ample opportunity.

Harry was anxious for the coming confrontation as he walked up the neatly manicured brick path that led to the house of his next-door neighbors, Sue and Phil Martin.

24

Flushed with excitement, he pressed the doorbell, wondering what their reaction would be when they answered it and saw him standing there. His speculations, however, were cut short. As the doorbell rang, it triggered the image of the pealing bells in the tower, and then, immediately, as if the two were somehow connected, the fountain appeared again. Only, this time the building behind it was no longer a vague outline. This time it was clearly visible, its address spelled out in flowing script above the entrance.

The sound of a half-stifled gasp of surprise brought Harry back to the present, and he saw Sue Martin standing in front of him in the open doorway. For a moment the two simply looked at each other.

"Hello, Sue. Can I come in?"

"Of course, but . . ."

"But what?"

"Carol said you were in the hospital, that you were very ill."

"We can talk about it inside."

Embarrassed and a little afraid, Sue stepped aside and let him in. Just then Phil was heard from the living room.

"Who is it, honey?"

"It's Harry." Sue's voice came close to breaking when she said his name.

Phil hurried into the entry hall. "For Christ's sake, we thought you were in the hospital. When did you get out?"

"Just this evening."

"You feel okay? What was wrong with you, anyway?"

“Why don’t we go into the living room, where we can be comfortable?” Sue said, attempting to regain her composure.

As the three of them moved through the entry hall, Harry remembered that Phil’s car was parked in the driveway and took note out of the corner of his eye that the keys were in their usual place, on top of a small, intricately carved credenza.

“How about a drink?” Phil asked.

“Scotch and water,” Harry said as he sat down in a gold armchair.

“Anything for you, hon?”

“I think I could use one,” she said.

“Right. Be back in a sec.”

She settled herself on the end of the sofa farthest from Harry. For once, he had the psychological edge, and he was hoping to use it to his advantage.

“So Carol told you I was in the hospital.”

“Yes; she said you’d been taken ill up at that resort.”

“Tarawaulk Bay.”

Sue nodded nervously. “We certainly didn’t expect to see you so soon.”

“Really?”

“Well, I mean from what she said, it was nip and tuck. But you look fine.”

“Carol tends to exaggerate. You should know that.”

“I’m glad she did.”

“Hey, Sue,” Phill called out from the kitchen, “we got any peanuts or anything around?”

“In the cupboard over the dishwasher,” she called back. Then, to Harry: “Maybe I’d better go and help him.”

“I’m sure he’ll manage. Stay where you are.” Sue obeyed, shifting uneasily on the sofa.

Phil entered carrying the three drinks in a wedge formation, a silver-plated nut dish dangling precariously from the little finger of his right hand. Harry took his drink and waited until Phil was seated before raising his glass in a toast.

“To my unexpected recovery,” he said mockingly, the image of the building behind the fountain still vivid in his memory.

"So tell us what the hell happened to you," Phil said. "And where's Carol? Doesn't she know you're out?"

"Interesting questions, aren't they?" Harry's reply made Phil uncomfortable.

"Listen, if you don't want to talk about it, it's okay with me."

"Oh, I want to talk about it, Phil. I just want to be the one asking the questions."

"Like what?"

"Like where's my wife? And why is my house for sale, gutted of every stick of furniture?"

"Don't you know?" Sue asked, genuinely sincere.

"Obviously not."

She looked at her husband, who picked up the conversation.

"Early this morning we got a phone call from Carol. She sounded very upset and told us that you'd become seriously ill up in New England and that she'd had to rush you to a hospital. She said you were in a coma and that it could be weeks or even months before you were well again. She knew your insurance wouldn't cover the medical expenses, so she was putting the house on the market and moving the furniture into storage until she could find an apartment and then sell what she didn't need."

Sue continued. "Around ten this morning a man came to put up the For Sale sign, and a little while later the movers arrived and took away the furniture."

"What was the name on the van?" Harry asked.

"I'm not sure. Consolidated . . . Continental, something like that. I remember it began with a C."

"What about Carol; have you heard from her since this morning?"

"Look, don't misunderstand this," Phil said, "but she's *your* wife. Why should you have to come here for information?"

"Because I haven't seen her since I . . . since I was taken ill."

The Martins didn't bother to conceal their suspicion. "Surely she must have been with you in the hospital," Sue said.

"No."

"Now, wait a minute." Phil was getting annoyed at Harry's answers. "Just what are you trying to say? That Carol dumped you in a hospital, left you in a coma, and never bothered to check on you?"

"I was never in a coma, and I haven't seen Carol since sometime after twelve-thirty this morning."

"C'mon, Harry; talk sense."

"I am."

There was an ungainly pause before Sue spoke.

"How did you get here? Carol must have the car."

"I hitched."

"All the way from New England?"

The momentum had shifted. They were the ones with the advantage now, and Harry abruptly stood up to leave. "Thanks for the drink."

"Aren't you forgetting something?" Phil's tone was slightly condescending, as if he were speaking to a precocious child.

"The car," Sue said reasonably. "You don't have a car. Carol sent the extra one to a garage, somewhere."

Harry was getting nervous, and he could feel the beginnings of a headache. "I'll call a cab and go to a motel."

"Listen, why don't you spend the night here? Who needs a motel room?" Phil's voice was gentle, coaxing.

"Really, it's no trouble at all," Sue added.

"Thanks, but I'm a lousy houseguest. I'd be more relaxed by myself."

"Okay," Phil said, "if that's what you want, I'll call you a cab. So sit down and finish your drink."

Harry made an awkward move back to the chair, and Phil walked to the bedroom to make the call.

"It'll probably take the cab at least ten or fifteen minutes to get here," Sue said, but her comment went unanswered.

There was a wall phone just a few steps away in the kitchen. Why had Phil chosen to make the call in the privacy of the bedroom?—unless he was going to talk to someone other than the cab company.

The headache sprang full force on Harry, the pain climbing up the back of his head. He reached out for his drink, but before his hand touched the glass the pain vanished and the Martins' living room was supplanted by a flash of J. McNeal's office door. Only, this time it stood open. Wide open. And McNeal was sitting behind his desk, his face in plain view.

It was the face of Harry Milford.

25

The mirror image faded, and Harry was returned once again to the Martins' living room, shattered by the revelation he'd just witnessed. His face had the glaze of a shellshocked combatant.

"Harry?" Sue's voice seemed to be coming from a great distance away.

"Harry, what's wrong? Shall I call a doctor?"

He turned to look at her. She sounded honestly concerned, but he had been tricked before. He could no longer afford to trust anyone.

"Good-bye, Sue."

"But what about the cab?" Looking at Harry, Sue had the uncanny feeling that she no longer knew him.

"I won't be needing it. And you can tell Phil that whoever he's talking to, he's wasting his time."

Harry stood up and walked quickly out of the room and into the entry hall. Sue's first impulse was to call for her husband, but then she decided to follow Harry and turned the corner just in time to see him grab the car keys from the credenza and open the front door.

"Phil! Phil, come here!"

By the time she'd called for help, Harry was already out the door and sprinting toward the car. As he ran, he felt for the squared corners of the ignition key and held it at the ready. Sliding it into the lock, he heard the agitated voices of Phil and Sue coming from the house, and then the sound of someone running down the walk.

"Harry! For Christ's sake, stop it!"

He slammed the door and jammed the key into the ignition. Simultaneously, the engine kicked over and the seat-belt buzzer blared out its warning. Phil was only one or two strides from the car as Harry shifted into reverse and lurched out of the driveway. Then the transmission thumped into gear, and he was gone, leaving behind him the stench of burning rubber and the sudden, overwhelming stillness of the night.

"Shit" Phil said. "He's crazy."

Sue was now standing beside her husband on the front lawn. "Did you get through to Carol?"

"Just barely. I only got to tell her he was here when the damn fool took off. I'm going to call the police."

"Don't."

"Why the hell not? He stole our car."

"I know, but we're supposed to be his friends. That's why Carol left us that number; we owe it to her to talk to her first."

"And what about her? Didn't she owe us the courtesy of the truth instead of that crap about him being in a coma? I mean, what the hell, the guy's obviously escaped from the hospital."

Sue's tone was calm and reasoning, trying to cut through her husband's anger. "Phil, I don't know what's wrong with Harry, any more than you do. But I'm sure Carol told us what she thought was best. Maybe he's had some kind of a breakdown and she's trying to keep it quiet. Can you blame her for wanting to protect her husband?"

"I guess not. All right, I'll call her. But I'm telling her I'm going to report the stolen car. In his condition, he could turn the thing into a weapon."

She nodded her agreement, and together they walked back to the house.

The din of the seat-belt buzzer was infuriating. Harry pulled to the side of the road and buckled up, stopping the relentless noise. The quiet in its wake was almost audible.

He looked at his two hands resting on the steering wheel

and felt no connection with them whatsoever. In fact, he felt as if he no longer knew anything about himself at all. Who was he? Harry Milford, or J. McNeal? Which was reality and which fantasy? Or were they both real, one intertwined with the other? He knew very well that he could sit there all night asking himself such questions, and he also realized that any delay was merely an act of cowardice. Because now he knew where to find the answers. They were waiting for him in the building behind the beautiful fountain—the building in Washington, D. C.

Almost hesitantly he pressed the accelerator and drove away.

When Harry pulled up in front of the Washington office building, a drizzly rain was beginning to fall and his body ached from the tension of the trip. He knew that as soon as he'd hit the thruway he'd been followed—at a discreet distance, of course. At first he'd thought of trying to lose them, but he simply didn't have the spirit for it. If they wanted him dead, they would see to it, one way or the other, so what would be the point of prolonging the inevitable for an extra night or two? That could hardly be called living. No, he'd decided to drive straight to Washington and let them do whatever they wanted. When it was all over, he'd be either dead or alive; it was that basic. But at least he'd have learned what had been going on. Or he prayed that he would. The prospect of dying with his questions unanswered was the only thing that frightened him.

As he got out of the car, the peal of a bell cut through the soft patter of the rain. He looked diagonally across the street, and there, a majestic anachronism amid the modern buildings, stood a venerable old church and the bell tower that had invaded Harry's life so often during the past several days. The bells continued to toll the hour for about thirty seconds, and he watched their swaying movement with a clinical curiosity. In the abstract, they had been a nerve-wracking, unexplainable phenomenon. But now, in reality, it was like seeing the superstructure of some grotesque Hollywood monster—the terrifying reduced to the mechanical.

Once the bells had stopped, he turned his attention to the office building. The grandeur of the fountain was dulled by the depressing rain, and as he walked past, a gust of wind blew the mist from the water jets against his skin. Resolutely he climbed the low-slung concrete steps that led to the entrance. Even though it was well after business hours, it didn't surprise him to find the door unlocked. Sutherland, whoever he was, had already proved that he could accomplish anything.

Harry's feet sank into the plush gold carpeting as he walked across the deserted lobby to the bank of elevators. With an unhurried motion he pressed the car-call button, and a door immediately slid open before him. He stepped inside, turned around, and pressed the button for the twenty-second floor.

The ride was a swift one, and soon the doors were opening, the number twenty-two glowing bright red on the elevator panel, just as it had in the nightmare.

A long, empty corridor stretched out in front of Harry.

He didn't remember leaving the elevator. The first thing that registered with him was the number on the office door to his right: 2212. He began to move slowly down the center of the corridor, noting the descending numbers as he went—2209, 2207, 2206, 2203, 2202 . . . 2201.

There was no name on the door.

He could see the spot where the name plaque should have been, its outline still visible. Then he lowered his hand to the doorknob, knowing it would be unlocked. He gave it a turn and pushed inward, letting the momentum carry it open. Reaching inside, he switched on an overhead light. The fluorescent tubes flashed once or twice, then glowed brightly. Save for the squat shape of a black telephone resting on the floor near the window, the room was empty.

The veins in his temples began to throb. It was totally unfair—more than that, it was cruel—to let him come this far and be denied his final answers.

"Sutherland! Damn you! Show yourself!" His rage was swallowed up by the empty corridor.

Looking back into the office, he walked inside. It felt right; he'd been here before; he was sure of it. Crouching down, he saw that the furniture impressions were still deep in the carpet, making it easy for him to visualize the placement of the various pieces.

But why leave him dangling like this?

The shrill ring of the telephone filled the vacant room and sent a chill of anticipation through Harry. He stood up, advancing on the black instrument as if it were some malevolent presence. He wanted to pick it up quickly, but his body wouldn't obey, and he slowly knelt down beside it. His fingers had just gripped the receiver when suddenly the office door slammed shut behind him.

Harry sprang up, whirled around, and froze at what he saw. He was face-to-face with his wife. He flinched involuntarily as Carol raised the gun with its bloated silencer and fired point-blank at his chest.

The pain was followed by a sinking sensation, and Harry's body crumpled to the floor beside the ringing telephone.

26

Harry had been awake for almost ten minutes, lying in bed amid the familiar surroundings of his room at the New England clinic. How many hours had passed since Kathy had aided him in his "escape"? Precious few. But then, he reasoned, that was just as well. He was grateful that the final pieces of the puzzle had rushed swiftly into place, because now it was over. Now he remembered.

He reached for the bedside switch and raised himself to a sitting position. His chest ached from being shot. One of Sutherland's new toys, no doubt. He'd be interested to learn what it was. But that would come soon enough. He was certain of a visit from the dapper British-American whose reigning position in the upper echelons of intelligence had gone unchallenged for more than fifteen years.

And what would Harry say to him? Right now he was a volatile mixture of frustration, anger, and relief. It ought to make for a most interesting meeting.

There was a brisk knock on the door, and a distinguished-looking gray-haired gentleman with angular features entered the room.

"Hello, Sutherland."

"Welcome home, Harry."

"I could say your hospitality stinks, but I won't."

"My, we're a bit peevish, aren't we?"

"Pissed off, would be a whole lot closer."

"I suppose I can understand that."

"Don't be sympathetic. It doesn't become you."

"Perhaps you're not up to our little talk."

"As a matter of fact, I've been looking forward to it." He rubbed his hand over his sore chest. "What the hell did she shoot me with, anyway?"

"Tranquilizer projectile. Most effective, don't you think?"

"Do you know what I'd like to do? I'd like to take you and your toys, mount you in cement, and dump you in the deepest river I could find."

"Now, Harry . . . "

"Cut out the crap. My name's McNeal. James McNeal."

Sutherland raised a bushy white eyebrow and slid a hand into the pocket of his impeccably tailored blue blazer.

"So, you *are* beginning to remember. The question is, how much?"

Harry thought back over the wild course of events he'd been through. "Everything," he said.

"That covers a great deal of territory. Supposing you give me a for-instance."

"Okay. For instance: Carol isn't my wife. She's one of your operatives, assigned to keep an eye on me while I was away from the Maryland agency. How's that for openers?"

"You always did enjoy leading with a strong card. But why should we be interested in your comings and goings?"

"Come on, Sutherland, the game's over; we both know that. Now, let's get to the problems at hand."

"The game, dear boy, won't even begin to be over until you've convinced me you know why you're here."

"And you're going to make me do it the hard way."

"The *only* way, James. Which means that I'm going to stand here and listen patiently while you debrief yourself. I intend to give you no help, and to answer only those questions that imply no revelation of your past history. Is that quite clear?"

"You've made your point."

"Good. Please begin."

Harry felt like a schoolboy appearing before his professor

to recite some memorized lines; only, this time he was both author and subject.

"My name is James McNeal. Until approximately six months ago, I was the first chief of a newly formed intelligence-coordinating agency. My position gave me access to a large number of top-secret documents—documents which might not be declassified for many years.

"Since the first rule of concealment is simplicity, I operated under the cover of an ordinary businessman in a typical Washington high rise. All classified information was, of course, handled in code, and there was a scramble system on my phone, but other than that I was very open and accessible. I even had my name on the door for everyone to see."

Harry envisioned that same office, stripped of its furnishings, where his search had ended only a few hours before.

"Something the matter?" Sutherland asked.

"Why did you clean out the office?"

"Later. You haven't finished yet."

"Damnit! You owe me an explanation!"

"And you'll have it. In the meantime, I believe you were saying something about your cover."

"Fuck it."

Sutherland bowed his head in concentration and took one or two steps toward the door before looking back up at Harry.

"Although I could, I don't intend to force you to tell me anything. But perhaps I should clarify your position. If you don't remember exactly who you were and what you did as James McNeal, then you leave me no other choice than to consider you a prime security risk. And you're enough of a professional to know what that means."

Harry thought about calling his bluff, then decided against it. The safe thing to do was talk.

"In order to protect my cover, we couldn't let it be associated with me for too long. So after two years I was 'retired,' and someone else was to move in to take my place—different man, different name, different occupation. A simple change of tenants; happens all the time in a big building like that."

Harry reached for a glass of ice water beside his bed. "You wouldn't have anything I could add to this, would you?"

"I'm afraid that's up to the doctors."

"For once in your life, do something nice. I need a drink."

"I'm listening, James, but I don't hear anything. Now, what was all this about your retiring from your job?"

Harry set the water glass down with a sharp bang.

"As soon as I was pulled from the position, I became our number-one problem. I'd obviously seen and heard more than enough to make me vulnerable, but we couldn't advertise the fact that I had one of the highest security clearances in the country by suddenly surrounding me with protection. So we decided to give me a new life, and that's where Dr. Ordway and his boys came in. He must have jumped at the chance to work on a healthy agent instead of the usual parade of gunshot wounds and neuroses the government keeps sending him. But I'll tell you something. I managed to develop a profound dislike for the man in a very short space of time."

"Spare me your editorials," Sutherland said. "That's not why I'm here."

"You needed a guinea pig for a new amnesia drug that was being perfected, and I fit the bill perfectly. Since I was single, with no living relatives, and few, if any, close friends, there'd be a minimum of explaining to do when I dropped out of sight. Besides, what better way to short-circuit my knowledge than to wipe it out entirely? I agreed, so you brought me here to the Company clinic and gave me the drug. Then Ordway and his assistants began the task of reengraving my mind. Using psychodrama, hypnotism, and the constant repetition of the facts of my new life as Harry Milford, you programmed me just like a computer."

The mention of the words caused him to recall the image of the computer tapes he'd been unable to explain.

"When the job was done," Harry continued, "you transplanted me to Maryland, where I wouldn't be likely to run into anyone who'd known me as McNeal. Carol would help see to that. And damned efficiently, too."

"We hire only the best, James. You know that."

"I suppose that once she realized that the drug was going bad, wearing off in patches, she was in constant touch with you?"

"Almost daily," Sutherland replied. "She kept me posted via telephone, usually from a public booth. We'd never use the same number twice."

"She's a cool one," said Harry.

"Yes, usually. She's asked for a brief vacation before her next job. You seem to have tired her a bit."

Harry looked up, but Sutherland's face remained impassive. So that was his last word on Carol.

"How about Sue and Phil?"

"Total innocents."

"What about the people at the Maryland office? Did they know who I really was?"

"Only Hastings. The others were simply told to report any unusual actions on your part."

"So I was being watched twenty-four hours a day."

"Absolutely."

"You complacent son-of-a-bitch! Why didn't you bring me in and reprogram me?"

Sutherland remained infuriatingly calm. "We could have, but we decided it would be to our advantage to observe your reactions—under controlled conditions, of course."

"You mean *you* decided. It must have been a lot of laughs watching me squirm, knowing that while I thought I might be losing my mind, I was actually gaining it back. That must have appealed to your sense of the ironic."

"Call it what you like. The fact of the matter is that you presented us with a unique opportunity to observe an agent's reactions in bizarre, life-threatening situations while under partial influence of the drug, at the point when his two different realities are in conflict. You've provided us with some startling new insights into brainwashing. In short, we did what we had to do."

"Like hell!"

"You knew from the beginning that you were to be a guinea pig; there was never any guarantee the drug was foolproof. Since it was malfunctioning anyway, we wanted to see if your fighting instincts would remain intact. We knew they were strong—you'd already tried to escape once during the programming."

The nightmare sequence of Harry's flight along the beach was vivid in his mind.

"You screwed that one up," he said to Sutherland. "You didn't reflect the ankle scar on my medical records. Sloppy move."

"A slipup on our part. Your physical description was copied from your original dossier."

Harry's anger had cooled, and the professional in him wanted some answers.

"Now it's my turn to do the asking."

"Go ahead," Sutherland said.

"Why did you pull Carol from the game?"

"Quite frankly, to see if it would send you over the edge. There were those who were betting it would."

"Who? Ordway?"

"It makes no difference. However, I thought you'd be determined to follow things through to the end. And you did. So you see, you're more than a guinea pig now, you're a precedent."

"Thanks a hell of a lot, but I can live without your applause."

Sutherland casually shrugged, took out a slim gold case, and began tamping down a cigarette with no filter.

"Still smoking those Turkish stink bombs?"

"Old habits are hard to break." He put back the case and lit up with a matching gold lighter.

"I know of one you managed to break."

"Oh?"

"Diane Kinney."

Sutherland's reaction was one of mild interest. "What do you remember about her?"

"She was a courier for us; her cover as a fashion model gave her the mobility she needed. Just before I retired, she came under suspicion of being a double agent."

"The suspicion was eventually confirmed. We leaked some obsolete information to her, which she dutifully passed on to her other employers. It took them several months to discover what we'd done to them. At that point, they could no longer afford to trust Ms. Kinney."

"So you set her up for the kill at Tarawaulk Bay, knowing I'd be there and that I was familiar with her face from her dossier and the magazine cover and wondering if meeting her would jog my memory."

"Well thought out," Sutherland said.

"You're damn lucky I didn't wind up dead along with her. Or was that what you were hoping for, to toss the other side a bonus?"

"Not at all. We knew they wouldn't touch you. Diane was an enemy to everyone; you were presumably an allied agent. Why should they kill a friend? We're in the era of detente, remember?"

"You're a devious bastard. You must have scared the shit out of that poor manager at the Bay—a dead body in one of his cottages, the government swearing him to secrecy."

"That particular manager happens to be a very good friend of ours."

Harry took another swallow of water and then drained the glass. "So now we come down to the big problem—me."

For the first time, Sutherland looked a bit uncomfortable.

"Odd, isn't it? If I had cracked up out there, you wouldn't have anything to worry about. You could just shovel me into a mental institution and forget about me."

Sutherland took a deep drag on his cigarette and exhaled the smoke slowly. "James, supposing I told you that you can't hurt us at all?"

"I'd say you were crazy. I saw documents; I discussed plans. A little sodium pentothal and we'd be an instant target for international blackmail, or worse."

Sutherland continued to look troubled. "A little while ago you wanted to know why we'd cleaned out your old office. Well, the answer is, we didn't. We haven't used it since you retired. It was empty when you got there merely by coincidence."

"So you've changed locations. So what?"

"No, James, we haven't changed locations. In fact, in a manner of speaking, we never had one to begin with."

"Wait a minute. What are you trying to tell me?"

"That it was all a dry run for the purpose of testing the drug. The information you accumulated during those two years is perfectly harmless."

Harry couldn't believe what he was hearing. He waited for Sutherland to laugh and betray the terrible joke, but he heard only the heavy rise and fall of his own breathing.

It was the truth.

"You set me up." He was surprised at the evenness of his tone, and he knew it wouldn't last.

"I'm sorry."

"You set me up! For two years I walked around sick with the knowledge I carried in my head! I lost count of the nights I couldn't sleep for fear of wondering what would happen if someone penetrated my cover and grabbed me! Two years, Sutherland! And you're 'sorry'?"

"I don't blame you, but try to see it our way. We had to have someone who was the logical choice for the job."

"Blow it out your ass. If you just wanted me to test the goddamn drug, you could have told me."

"You were the first person to receive such a massive dose. We weren't sure what effects it might have. And if it was to be useful at all on future agents, you had to *believe*—not only in your life as Harry Milford, but in your importance as James McNeal."

The moment arrived when all Harry wanted was to get his hands on Sutherland's throat. The impulse came close to settling into cold, hard resolve; and then, by subtle degrees, it changed course, and the perverse beauty of how efficiently he'd been used began to overtake him. As much as he disliked it, he had to admit it was one hell of a smooth con. The best. There was just one thread slightly loose.

"Wait a minute, Sutherland. You mean to tell me you footed the bill for two years of ball-point pens, executive lunches, and very high-class letterheads just because you trusted I'd agree to be the guinea pig? I didn't have to volunteer, you know. That whole setup could have been a great waste of the taxpayers' money."

"Let's just say we had faith in you." Sutherland smiled.

Harry smiled back at him. "You would have shot me full of it anyway, you son-of-a-bitch, even if I didn't volunteer."

"Come now, do you think I'm a barbarian?"

"You're forgetting, Sutherland. I remember you now."

"And do you remember this?"

Sutherland slipped his hand inside his blazer and withdrew a thick envelope, which he tossed onto the bed.

Harry tapped it with his finger, then pushed it away.

"Unless it's money, I don't want to see it."

"It's money—tied to a few conditions."

"Such as?"

"Your willingness to make yourself available for further experiments with the drug."

"You should have run for Congress, Sutherland. You've got monumental gall."

"I'm flattered."

"Don't be. There's no way on earth I'm going to sign that thing."

"We both know you're a gambler, James. But do as you

like. However, I'd read it if I were you. Especially the part with the dollar sign. At any rate, the offer's good for only forty-eight hours, so don't agonize too long over your decision."

"You stink, you know that?"

"Unfortunately, it comes with the territory. Good day, James."

Sutherland closed the door softly behind him.

Alone in the room, Harry laced his fingers behind his neck and leaned back against the pillow, the unopened envelope resting on his lap.

He was determined not to look at it. This time around, they could damn well find another pigeon for their game. He'd had enough. He just wanted a long vacation with nothing to do. Although he couldn't deny it would be nice to have the satisfaction of knowing how much Sutherland thought he was worth.

Grudgingly he reached for the envelope and removed the contract. He quickly scanned the legal language and then stopped short midway down a page.

It was a hell of a lot of money.